D1526158

TWO FRIENDS AND A FUNERAL

Wendy Dalrymple

Cover design by: Kateryna Dronova
Library of Congress Control Number: 2018675309
Printed in the United States of America

CONTENTS

CHAPTER ONE

Amy Grimes stood on the balcony of her Vero Beach condo watching the sun rise over a sparkling expanse of navy blue sea. It was just after 7:00 a.m. and she had already checked off all the boxes on her morning routine: a two-mile jog on the beach, shower, skincare regimen, and coffee. Amy twisted her long brunette locks up into the kind of bun that meant she was ready for business and opened her laptop to get started for the day. Her work queue was full and she had a dozen emails requiring her attention, including one from a new client and one from her accountant. Amy settled into her chaise lounge overlooking her waterfront view, cozied up to her favorite cashmere throw and smiled. Despite the long list of work she had lined up, Amy knew it was going to be a good and productive week.

Business had been pretty great for Amy the past four years — better than great, in fact. Things were going so well that she had recently been courted by not one but two tech companies to purchase her LLC. Considering that she was just a little girl from the backwoods of River Ranch, Florida, her nearly million-dollar business and paid-with-cash condo overlooking an expanse of powdery white, palm tree-lined Atlantic shores was nothing short of a miracle. Amy appreciated and enjoyed her hard-earned status every day and loved every inch of her ultra-modern home, from her walk-in closet stocked with designer clothes to her stark white furniture and clean aesthetic. Amy's perfectly curated corner of the world was literally and metaphorically miles away from the world she knew as a child. Though she loved her family and their messy, ancient home tucked away in the Central Florida woods, growing up, she always knew that she was destined for silk, leather, and highrises with a view.

Amy sighed contentedly as she weeded through her inbox and fielded an array of requests for adding new clients to her innovative online security platform. The patented ViruSmart technology she had developed in college catapulted her to success in the IT world, bringing her a small amount of notoriety and a decent amount of wealth well before her thirtieth birthday. Her condo in Vero Beach was only one of three properties Amy bounced between throughout the year, and was as much a symbol of her freedom as it was a symbol of her success.

After an hour of closing out tickets and responding to customers, Amy readjusted the elastic of her chestnut-brown bun and stretched in the early morning sunlight. Her head was still focused on her work, but her heart was already in Belize, where she would soon be snorkeling with her personal assistant and ride-or-die travel partner-in-crime Tausha. It had been a solid six months since she and Tash had gotten away together, and she knew her best girlfriend and most trusted employee would be happy for a few sun-soaked days away from the responsibilities of family life. Unlike Tausha, Amy could essentially pick up and go whenever and wherever she wanted without having a husband or other responsibilities to think about, and that was just the way she liked it.

Just as Amy was about to take a break for the morning, a new message appeared in her email and caught her attention. She took a sip of coffee and clicked back to her email tab and saw a name in her inbox that always made her smile.

Owen Durant.

Her oldest friend from back home was a tech professional just like she was, but unlike herself, Owen still held on to his country roots with two closed, calloused fists. He was an enigma in that way, and the idea of him splattered in mud from riding his ATV while solving intricate IT security issues always made her laugh. Owen wasn't usually one to email — in fact, *she* was usually the one to reach out to *him* — so seeing his message instantly caught her attention. But it wasn't his name in her inbox that made her do a double blink. Instead it was the subject line.

RE: Uncle LeRoy's Funeral
Uncle LeRoy!

Amy instantly knew that the contents of the email were bound to be a big deal. Owen's Uncle LeRoy was something of a local celebrity in Central Florida, with a voice and a face that everyone in their county recognized. A day wouldn't go by during her childhood without being exposed to the leader of the Durant family, as his likeness was plastered all over billboards, on the radio, or on television. The commercial tagline for their combination cattle, citrus, and timber business "Gettin' it Done with Durant " set to the tune of a twangy pop country song was an earwig that haunted Amy to this day. LeRoy's wide, toothy grin was always prominently featured front and center on Durant company advertisements and the image was permanently engraved in her memory. Uncle LeRoy was dead? How could that be?

Owen. With his classic Florida boy farmer's tan, penchant for boots and baseball caps, and appreciation for all things outdoors, it was hard for some people to see how he and Amy had anything in common. Amy's own Tory Burch dresses and Versace heels wouldn't stand a chance at the Durant family ranch these days. Even though Owen knew his stuff when it came to IT and kept the tech side of his family business running Monday through Friday, on the weekends, she knew he was happiest slogging through the forest, sitting atop an ATV, or relaxing by a fire pit. Their stark difference in interests and lifestyle choices endeared him to her and put a definitive pin in any possibility of romance between them all at the same time.

After a moment of hesitation, Amy finally clicked on the email and prepared herself for what it might say. She was only slightly annoyed that Owen decided to email her about something so sensitive in the first place, but then again, that's just the type of thing Owen would do. *A call would be nice now and then,* she grumbled to herself as she read the contents of the email. She smiled, glad to be hearing from her old friend just the same.

The note was brief, as all communication from Owen Durant typically was, and simply asked for her to call him when she wasn't busy. The note also hinted that her presence at Uncle LeRoy's funeral would be appreciated. Amy had grown up on the Durant property as the scrawny kid next door that his wealthy family took in like a stray cat. It had been more than ten years since Amy had set foot on the estate, but with the Durant family being ViruSmart's number one customer, she and Owen had stayed in regular contact through the years. They would grab a beer when she came home for the holidays and while she would have loved to have invited him to stay at one of her many investment properties, he chose not to venture far from the comforts of his cushy country home. It had occurred to Amy on more than one occasion that if Owen would just allow himself to enjoy places other than Central Florida every now and then, maybe things could be more than just friendly between them.

Amy closed her eyes and cast her mind back to those hot as hell summer days spent with Owen. Hours would pass in the blink of an eye as they tore around the pine scrub forest surrounding his family property, then cooled off in their pool until Amy's grandparents called her home. She was more adventurous back then and didn't mind getting a few scraped knees or stings from bees. Maybe she really liked stomping around in the woods when she was younger, or maybe she just liked being near Owen. Later there was one summer in particular when their high-fives suddenly turned into hand-holding, followed by a few stolen moments behind the stables and a shared kiss under the stars. She shook away the memory of one particularly hot and heavy Fourth of July so many summers ago as she picked up her phone and automatically dialed the number she knew so well. Even though their brief teenage encounter was half a lifetime ago, those memories lingered in her mind and always brought heat to her cheeks whenever she allowed herself to reminisce on them.

Amy knew she didn't have to go to the funeral, but she was keenly aware that if Owen was asking for her to come, things must be pretty bad. She picked up her phone and dialed, listening as it rang exactly three times before the husky drawl that could only belong to Owen Durant mumbled, "Hello?" in her ear. She bit her lip and paused before greeting him and bracing herself for whatever he had to say. Amy had no way of knowing it at the time, but the death of LeRoy Durant had set in motion a chain of events that would change her life forever.

CHAPTER TWO

Owen Durant absent-mindedly kicked the dirt loose from the treads of his boot as he stared at the laptop screen in front of him. It was a Monday morning in early February — a cool, clear fifty-eight degrees — and he wanted nothing more than to crack open his new paintball gun and test it out in the woods behind his home office. He would rather be fishing out at DeSoto lake or even driving his family's prized Black Angus cattle clear across the acres of Durant property with his younger brother Dominic. He would rather be doing just about anything other than staring at a screen again on that fine Florida winter morning. But before he could even dream of tromping off into his beloved woods, Owen had a few loose ends to tie up with work, and an important email to send out. An email that was *not* going to be easy to explain.

Uncle LeRoy's death didn't exactly come as a surprise to everyone in the Durant family. The old codger had been living off oxygen and borrowed time for the past year, keeping everyone on his will in suspense. Owen knew he should have felt more remorse at his uncle's passing... hell, *everyone* should have felt more remorse. But LeRoy Ashley Durant Jr. wasn't exactly an easy person to get along with and was even more difficult to please and impress. While Owen knew he was his Uncle LeRoy's favorite nephew, even he wasn't immune to the infamous wrath of their family figurehead. Owen knew he would need to act fast if he was going to take over his uncle's shares of the Durant family wealth, and that's where Amy Grimes would come in.

Amy.

Owen's childhood best friend-turned-business associate was the first and only person he would have ever considered for his scheme. What he was about to ask of her was highly inappropriate, bizarre, and possibly even illegal, and he knew that only Amy could be trusted to help him. If she said no, then everything that Owen had been working on for the past ten years would be for nothing.

After typing and then retyping the email, obsessively reading it and deleting and retyping it again, Owen finally settled on just the right wording. He was used to keeping his business communications brief, but this was not a quick note kind of situation. Owen knew he could call Amy, but he assumed she was probably busy and didn't want to disturb her. Amy was *always* busy. She could be out jogging or on the phone with a client or maybe even at the bottom of a cenote with a scuba tank on her back for all he knew. He didn't want to be a bother, and so a simple, obsessively crafted email would have to do.

Owen exhaled heavily through his nose and sent the email with his heart banging away in his chest. There was no way to get out of what he was going to ask her now. He didn't know what she would say when she eventually called, but hell, who would? It wasn't every day you called up the person you kissed fifteen summers ago, the same person who had since become one of your best friends and a whip smart business partner. It wasn't every day that you asked that person the biggest favor you would ask anyone in your entire life. It wasn't every day that....

She thinks my tractor's sexy!

Owen nearly jumped out of his skin as the tinny country song sliced the silence of his office. Amy's custom ringtone was something of an inside joke, but as he struggled to steady his heart, he wondered if maybe it was time to change the ringer on his phone. Amy Grimes and Kenny Chesney's lyrics had nearly given him a heart attack. He hit send on his email to her only a few minutes before and hadn't been expecting a call back so soon. Owen dusted the cobwebs away from his mind and focused as he grabbed his loud, obnoxious phone. It was go time.

"Hullo," he said, clearing his throat. "Amy?"

"Owen," she laughed on the other line. "Hi."

Owen took off his baseball cap and scratched the back of his head, running his hands through his newly cropped hair. He cleared his throat again and stared out the window, trying to stall for time. He didn't know how the *hell* he was going to do this.

"I'm sorry to hear about Uncle LeRoy," she finally said, filling the dead air on the line. "Are you doing okay?"

"Fine," he exhaled. "I'm fine, thank you. Thanks for calling back so soon."

"It's okay," she said, her voice softer now. "I saw the subject line and didn't want to wait. What's up?"

Owen cleared his throat again. How was he supposed to say what he needed to say? How was he supposed to actually ask her?

"Yeah, um. I was wondering... I mean I was hoping... you spent a lot of time around here growing up. LeRoy looked on you just like one of his nieces. I was just thinkin'...."

"Owen, I'm coming to the funeral, don't worry," she said, her voice soft and sweet in his ear. He closed his eyes and exhaled in relief.

"Thanks."

Another moment of silence passed between them on the line. He couldn't do it. He couldn't say it.

"I can come on Friday and stay the weekend," she started again. "I'll even take you out for a beer. It's been a while since we caught up anyway."

"Well," he said, clearing his throat again. "I was actually hoping you could come a little sooner than Friday."

Amy chuckled in his ear.

"I figured there might be something else."

He could practically see her shaking her head at him.

"I was hoping you could come on Wednesday... for the reading of the will."

Owen heard Amy crunching in the background.

"What for?" she said, around a mouthful of food. "I mean, if you need like, some moral support or something I'm there."

Owen sucked in a sharp breath.

"Maybe it would be better if you just got here and then I could tell you all about it over that beer?" he asked. "I know you're probably swamped, and it's a lot to ask, but I really need your help with something."

Amy stopped crunching on the other line.

"Sure thing then, O," she said. "The beauty and burden of working for yourself is that you can take your office anywhere. I'll have some work to finish up this week, but I've been meaning to come visit my folks anyway. I'll be there Wednesday."

Owen exhaled again and smiled for the first time that morning.

"Thanks, Ame."

"Meet me at The Watering Trough on Wednesday? Say about five?"

"You read my mind," he smiled into the phone. "It's a date."

Owen cringed at the word.

Why did my dumb ass have to say date?
"Sounds good, Durant. Bye."
"Bye."

Owen's temples throbbed as he tossed his phone back on the counter next to his despised laptop. The prospect of what was likely to unfold over the next few days had begun to set in and paralyze him. Frustrated, he closed up his computer and decided he had done enough for the day. He was allowed to take some time off to work out his thoughts. He was still mourning for his uncle, after all.

Owen geared up his new paintball gun, his face mask, and a loaded magazine of paintballs and opened the back door of his office. When he was having a tough day or was just frustrated with work, being able to stomp back into the woods and throw axes, shoot at aluminum cans, or take a quick spin on his ATV always made him feel better. The outdoors saved his sanity on a daily basis, but Owen knew that no amount of target practice or mudding would help him now. As he trudged toward the treeline that spilled into the expanse of the Durant family property, one thought, and one thought alone, dominated his head and his heart.

How was he actually going to convince Amy Grimes to marry him?

CHAPTER THREE

The tires on Amy's BMW crunched over the gravel driveway leading up to the modest three bedroom, one bath residence she used to call home. Not much had changed since she had moved out of her parents house right after high school; her tire swing still hung from the big oak in the front yard, her mother's creepy angel statue still stood guard by the front door, her dad's rusted shell of a 1970 VW beetle continued to deteriorate under a tarp in the driveway. The view was somehow comforting and triggering all at once.

The low howl of her mother's beagle, Cookie, sounded from the front window and the vertical blinds shook, signaling that Amy had been spotted. She pulled around to the back of her white Series 4 Coupe, popped the trunk, and retrieved her Louis Vuitton signature logo luggage. She had only packed her bandouliere duffle and laptop bag and was determined to stay until Saturday or Sunday at the most. It wouldn't take much for Rhonda and Jeff Grimes to entice her to stay longer, but unfinished business and a lack of clean laundry were always a good excuse to go home.

As Amy neared the front porch with her

$2,000 duffel at hand, her mother came into view in the doorway. It had only been a month since she had seen her family for Christmas, but they had all flown out to her Colorado condo to enjoy some holiday snow. Rhonda Grimes still looked much like she always had standing on the rickety front porch with her signature shaggy frosted bouffant of hair and cartoon character T-shirts. She clasped her hands together, displaying long, hot pink acrylic nails that shone under the dappled early morning sun, and her heavily lined eyelids shimmered with joy.

"*Aymeeee!*" her mother crooned, scooping her into a hug. "You're early!"

"Hi, mom," she mumbled into her mother's shoulder. "Sorry I didn't call."

"Oh, don't be sorry at all!" Rhonda exclaimed. She put two fingers between her teeth and let out a high, sharp whistle. "Jeff! Get your ass out here! Your daughter is home!"

Amy covered her ears a little too late at her mother's enthusiasm.

"Ouch, mom."

"Sorry, Pumpkin," her mom winced. "I swear, your dad is more hard of hearing than ever. When he starts shuffling around in that office of his…."

"There's our little Tater Tot."

Jeff Grimes slapped open the front screen door and walked slowly across the creaking front porch. Amy cringed internally as she listened to the buckling floorboards beneath the weight of her sizable father.

"Careful dad," she cautioned, and gave her mother a look.

"Oh, he's fine," Rhonda said, waving the situation off.

"Mom," she whispered. "I told you I would send someone out to fix the porch! Why won't you let me?"

"Amy, I told you, we're *fine!*" her mother insisted. "Your father and I will *not* have you spending your hard-earned money on us. No, ma'am. We can manage on our own, we always have."

"Come here, Sport," her dad huffed, wrapping her in a hug. The walk from the house to the driveway had winded him, reviving Amy's worry. "You stayin' for awhile?"

"Yeah, at least until the weekend," she said, following them into the house. "Owen asked me to go to his uncle's funeral."

"So LeRoy Durant finally kicked the bucket," her father chuckled, shaking his head.

"That's perfectly *awful*," her mother said, throwing Amy's father a scolding look. "Poor Owen. Does this mean he'll officially have more stake in the family business?"

"I don't know," Amy said, slinging her bag down on her parents' worn circular couch. Cookie the beagle licked her hand and began to sniff at the bag.

"I'm going to meet him for a beer this afternoon to talk about everything, I guess."

"Well, you're going to have lunch with us first, right?" her mother said, her face lined with worry. "I made a whole mess of chicken salad."

"Yeah, of course," Amy said, looking around her family home.

The tiny living room that once seemed so big to her was the size of her walk-in closet at the beach condo, and the walls needed a fresh coat of paint. Her 11x13 framed high school graduation photo was prominently featured over her mother's piano in the front room, right next to the artificial Christmas tree her parents still hadn't taken down. Piles of paperwork and bills stacked up, dusty and forgotten on the kitchen island that separated the living room from their dining space. Coming home was always hard for Amy, but staying away was even harder.

"Do you mind if I go lie down in my old room for a while?" Amy yawned. "I haven't been sleeping well and I don't want to look like death warmed over when I meet Owen."

"Nonsense, you're beautiful, Punkin," her father said, giving her a peck on the cheek. He wiped a thin layer of sweat from his brow and huffed, then slowly lowered himself into his favorite armchair.

"Thanks, Dad," Amy said, with a half smile, half frown.

"I just put on some fresh sheets, you go right ahead," her mother nodded, retreating to the kitchen. "I'll just make you a sandwich and stick it in the fridge when you're ready, okay?"

"Sounds good, Mom."

Amy slung her duffle on her shoulder and walked the ten familiar steps from the living room to her childhood bedroom. Though over a decade had passed, her parents had kept the space virtually the same as when she had gone off to college. Taylor Swift stared back at her from the far wall, seated cross-legged and holding a guitar with her hair still in long, spiraling curls. A banner from River Ranch High School hung over her white shaker style desk next to her corkboard of fashion magazine clippings, photos, ticket stubs, and mementos. Even her bookshelf was still filled with all the YA post-apocalyptic novels she had consumed in high school. The room was a time capsule, a strange memento of her past, and simply being there made her feel like she had traveled back in time.

Despite being surrounded by the embarrassing remnants of the person she used to be, Amy was utterly exhausted. She flopped down on her childhood twin bed. The white and yellow floral calico quilt felt soft and familiar beneath her fingertips. She closed her eyes and began to drift, but was unable to really get any sleep. There was an unnamed question on her mind that had kept her up, tossing and turning all night for the last two days. Something she couldn't quite put her finger on tugged at her heart, causing her to feel restless and unsettled. It was the feeling that something big was about to happen.

* * *

Amy arrived early at The Watering Trough later that afternoon and was instantly flooded with more good memories. She could count on one hand the number of times she and her girlfriends had been able to successfully sneak into the country-western bar when she came home from college to visit during breaks or for the holidays. The kitschy cowboy aesthetic made the establishment seem more like an adult theme park than a bar, from its mounted steer head over the beer tap to the stacks of hay bales in the corners, right down to the discarded peanut shells on the floor. The Watering Trough offered line dancing and mechanical bull rides Thursday through Saturday, and Monday through Wednesday was karaoke night. Sundays, it was closed; Lake County was still conservative, after all.

Even though Amy already knew her long-sleeved floral Erin Featherston dress was going to make her stick out amongst the sea of denim and plaid like a sore thumb, she still wanted to look nice and feel comfortable. It had been a while since she had seen Owen in person, and she needed their reunion to be... memorable. She couldn't help but hold a candle for him, even after so many years and all of the differences between them. Even if they wanted different things in life, time had never fully washed away their history and the way that she felt about him in her heart.

Amy ordered an Orange City Porter from the bartender, surprised to see that the local watering hole had added microbrews to the menu. The last time she had stepped foot in the bar was for Ashley Stigler's bachelorette party three years before and the best beer she could get back then was a Stella Artois. She thoughtfully sipped the dark, local brew and checked the time on her phone when the front door opened, spilling soft winter sunshine into the darkened bar.

Owen had arrived right on time at 5:00 p.m., just as they had agreed, and the sight of him from afar made her do a slight double take. He was still wearing his faded, frayed "Durant Farms" baseball hat (there was no separating him from that), but the crisp dark jeans and black button-down indicated that he made an effort for the meeting. Amy's eyes scanned her old friend, noting the changes since she had last seen him. A few more sprigs of silver sparkled at his temples and the laugh lines around his eyes were etched just a little deeper. His cheeks were kissed by the sun as always, and his outdoorsy activities had kept him lean and muscular. As he strode up to meet her, his dirty work boots and dazzling smile showed her that she was still dealing with the same old Owen Durant.

"Still drinking fancy beer, I see."

Amy rose and met her friend with a hug, breathing in his signature scent of sunshine and sweet spice.

"Still wearing your hat indoors, I see."

The scruff of his cheek brushed hers as they parted. She playfully tapped the bill of his hat and forced herself to look away. Hugging Owen Durant was usually no big deal. She hugged *all* of her friends. Amy was a hugger! But this hug felt different somehow. She realized that her face was growing warm and her head was a little buzzy, but she brushed it off as a side effect from the strong beer.

The two old friends took their seats at the bar and Owen ordered himself an Orange City Pilsner. They caught up on old times. When the bartender brought him his drink, Owen and Amy clinked glasses in remembrance of Uncle LeRoy. They continued to talk shop about VirusSmart clients and their IT woes, each of them ignoring the real reason for their meeting. Half their drinks were downed before Amy finally brought up the unspoken thing between them. The reason she was there in the first place.

"So, Owen..." She smiled, gently kicking him on the shins. "Tell me why you dragged me all the way out to River Ranch to sleep on my old twin bed two days early. And it better be good."

Owen closed his eyes and took a deep breath, his forehead lined with worry. It occurred to Amy that she remembered that look from long ago. It was an image that had burned into her memory of his face pained and panicked when she had fallen out of the old oak in his backyard when she was eleven. He looked scared. Something about the way he was looking at her reactivated that long buried memory and heightened her senses. In that moment, Amy knew something big was about to happen.

"Come on, O. Spill it."

Owen glanced at her with a strange sort of smile and looked away. He sat up and sucked in a deep breath of air with his back straight as a pole and his shoulders squared as he looked back at her again. Owen took off his baseball cap and reached across the bar, taking his hands in hers. His expression was dead serious.

"Amy," he said. "I was wondering if you would want to marry me."

CHAPTER FOUR

Owen recoiled in horror as Amy let out a loud, raucous laugh that echoed through the entire bar. Her cackle cut through the country-western music and the murmured din of the other patrons, so loud that it must have echoed all the way out the door, down Highway 27, and through the streets of downtown River Ranch. It was a laugh he normally loved, but in this case, her outburst felt like a knife to the heart. He scanned the sea of startled faces; to his horror, all eyes were on them.

"*Marry* you! What?"

"Shh, keep it down!" he whispered, his eyes darting around the room. "And why is that so funny?"

Amy continued to hug her sides, gasping for air as she tried to compose herself.

"This is a joke, right?"

"No. I mean it."

Amy doubled over with laughter and Owen could only watch and remain speechless as splotches of red dotted her neck and face. Even though he was a little insulted and her complexion was quickly turning scarlet, he couldn't stay too mad at her. She was still pretty cute when she laughed, even if it *was* at him.

"It's not going to be for *real*," he whispered. "If you'll stop hee-hawin' like a damn donkey I'll explain everything."

Amy let out a final sigh of laughter and took another sip of beer. She hiccupped and cleared her throat before she was finally able to settle down. She fanned herself with her hand and looked over at Owen who was very visibly pouting.

"So you want to get married, but not for real?" she whispered, still giggling. "Why on Earth would we want to do that?"

Owen rolled his eyes and leaned in, the tips of his ears turning red.

"*Because*," he hissed through gritted teeth. "If I don't get married, then I'm out of Uncle LeRoy's will."

"That's ridiculous," she said, sitting back in her seat.

"Well, LeRoy Durant was ridiculous. He told my father all about his expectations for me and the company before he died and then my father told me. I only just found out last week that this was literally his dying wish."

"So let me get this straight," she said, leaning forward again. "You want me to marry you so you can get your inheritance? Why me?"

Owen scratched the back of his head, retrieved his baseball cap and returned it to its rightful position. He gave her a half-frown again and sighed through his nose.

"Because you're the only one I could trust with something like this. Because I know you feel the same way about marriage as I do. And because you know my family, and they know you and it wouldn't come as such a surprise."

"Wait… but won't it seem obvious if we get married right after the reading of the will? Your family is sure to know we're just getting married so you can cash in," Amy said, sipping her beer.

"That's why we need to pretend like we're engaged *now*. Our family might catch on, but they won't say anything. Shoot, they all like you better than they like me. I'm sure they'll be thrilled."

"But this can't be *legal*."

"Listen, the only stipulation so far as I know is that I get married," Owen said, finishing off his own beer. "Uncle LeRoy owned land holdings as an entity of some church and he wanted to keep it that way. As you might recall he was *very* religious and for whatever reason, he thought I should be married before I take it on."

"I don't know," she said, her eyes narrowing. "That's a pretty ridiculous dying wish. This whole scheme seems dishonest."

"Well, it's either this or my share of the inheritance goes into escrow until I die. Katie and Dominic are already married with kids, so control of Uncle LeRoy's side of the business and estate will probably go to them."

Exasperated, Owen signaled to the bartender to bring them two more beers. Amy wriggled in her seat. She was literally and figuratively having a hard time sitting on this information.

" I mean, I really don't ever see myself wanting to get married to *anyone*," Owen continued. "But if Uncle LeRoy's will states what my father says it's going to say, this is the only way."

Amy's shoulders and eyes softened as Owen slumped in his chair. He had no idea how a conversation like this was supposed to go, but so far, it was *not* going well.

"I can't say I blame you," Amy said, holding her hands up defensively. "I'm not interested in getting married to anyone either."

Owen scrunched up his forehead and looked over at Amy. Her complexion wasn't quite as flushed as before.

"I'm such a dummy. I didn't even think to ask you if you were seeing anyone."

"I see a lot of people," Amy said, her eyebrows raised. She tapped her nails on her nearly empty beer bottle. "But I'm not seeing anyone in particular right now."

"Me neither," he nodded. "And I wouldn't expect you to stop doing what you do. I'm not asking for you to uproot your whole life just for me."

"Don't worry, I wouldn't," she smirked, raising her eyebrows again. "It's not my love life I'm worried about though. If I'm going to put my neck on the chopping block for you, I'm going to need a really good reason."

Owen closed his eyes and inhaled slowly.

"Look, I'm not just doin' this to get out of paying taxes or to make a quick buck," he explained. "I mean, I like nice things and I enjoy my freedom just as much as you do, but I'm done giving our land up to the church. I have other plans."

"Oh? Like what?" she said, leaning on the counter. "Making the world's largest ATV race track?"

"*No*," he said, throwing her a dirty look. "Although that would be pretty great."

"Well, what then?" she said, slapping the bar top. "Owen, you really have to persuade me if you're going to ask me to do something crazy like this."

Owen frowned and looked down at his nearly empty beer.

"Camp Durant. Well, that's what I want to call it. Maybe you can come up with something better."

"You want to open a camp?"

"Amy, I'm sick to death of working behind a computer. I have this idea for starting up a summer camp for at-risk youth right back in our family property. I can teach kids survival techniques and how to appreciate the outdoors... well, I mean, me and a bunch of experts, that is."

Amy blinked and stared at her beer. It was clear to Owen that this was *not* what she had expected to hear. An unsettled silence burrowed in between them as she continued to process the proposition.

"Well, I can't say I'm surprised," she said, peeling away the label on the beer bottle. "You're good at what you do, but I know you've been trying to get out of the IT world for a while."

"I just want to do something else with my life," he shrugged. "I want to do something worthwhile. What good is having all that land and money and not putting it to good use?"

Another moment of silence passed between them as they both thoughtfully sipped their beers. Owen used to be able to know exactly what Amy was thinking, but in this case, he couldn't tell.

"So, what's in it for me?" she finally asked, breaking the tension. "Why should I help you pull this off?"

Owen swallowed and raised his eyes to meet her gaze. His expression was serious and it took Amy aback, even more than his confession of wanting to abandon his IT career to essentially be a camp counselor.

"Half a million," he said, taking another swig of beer.

"Dollars?" she exclaimed. "You're going to give me half a million dollars just to get married?!"

"Shh, keep it down," he whispered, motioning with his hands. He looked around the mostly empty bar and continued to talk in a hushed tone.

"Yes," he said, softly. "Half a million dollars to get married and stay married until all of the assets are in my name and then a lifetime of discretion. River Ranch is a small town as you surely remember. Word travels fast."

Amy blinked.

"And then we just get the marriage annulled? No questions? Just like that?" she whispered.

"Yup."

Amy chugged her second beer, finishing it off in one long gulp and plunked the empty bottle on the bar.

"I could pay off my condo in Denver with that kind of money."

Owen nodded.

"Or I could just stash it away in my retirement portfolio and be set for life."

"Hell, you could finally sell ViruSmart and retire early if you really wanted to," he offered. "I mean, I know that you've been wanting to travel more. Here's your big chance."

She continued to give him *that look*. It was the look she always gave him when he was about to do something dangerous back when they were kids. Now he was asking her to come along for the ride and he didn't know if he could persuade her this time.

"Listen, Ame, I know it's a crazy plan, but it could help us both reach some major goals in a short amount of time."

Amy set her jaw, threw her shoulders back and stuck out her hand.

"Okay. Let's do this thing."

"Really?" he said, the worry instantly melting away from his face. "Are you sure?"

Amy nodded, eyes wide as she reached out to seal the deal with a handshake.

Owen accepted her outstretched hand and shook it up and down appreciatively. He looked down at their hands intertwined for a brief moment and a breath caught in his throat. He shook away the electric buzz that was racing up and down his spine and smiled despite the small grain of doubt that had settled into his gut.

"Yes, I'm positive," she said, gripping his hand even tighter. "Owen Durant, let's get married."

* * *

Amy settled their tab and the two friends spilled out into The Watering Trough's parking lot to face the chilly January night. A pitch black sky dotted with diamond stars hung overhead as they linked arms and headed toward their cars, talking and laughing all the way. Owen had conveniently parked his black mud-splattered F-150 next to her pristine new white sports coupe. When they reached their respective vehicles, Owen lowered the back flatbed of his truck and hopped up to take a seat. He patted the spot next to him and gave her a wicked grin.

"Come on. For old times' sake."

"It's freezing!" Amy protested, still laughing. She rubbed her arms and scooted onto the cold truck flatbed just the same.

"It's not that bad. Besides, we need to wait it out and sober up a bit anyway. Look at those stars."

Amy looked up into the moonless sky. It was indeed a nice night.

"Don't get skies like this in the city," she commented. "It's definitely one of the things I miss about living out here."

"Oh yeah? Miss Big Shot missing home a bit?" he joked, nudging her lightly with his elbow.

"*No*," she protested. "I am very happy to live far, far away from River Ranch where you don't have to drive for three hours to see a decent concert or sports game."

"Whatever," he said, rolling his eyes in the dark.

"You're going to have to get me a ring, you know," she mused. "If we are going to make this convincing, that is. We should probably set a date for the wedding too. People will ask."

"Oh," Owen frowned. "I hadn't thought of that."

"And we'll need to get a marriage license, find an officiant. Find a place to get married at the last minute…."

"Oh that part's easy. We can just have the wedding at the farm. My buddy Tucker can hook us up with an officiant too."

Amy nodded. "Okay. Well then, you just need to get a ring, and quick. I'm a size six. Oh, and no diamonds, make it something original, like a sapphire," she said, pulling out her phone. She quickly produced an image of a brilliant-cut blue square solitaire. Owen evaluated the image and frowned.

"Dang, Ame. How'm I s'posed to get something like this in River Ranch at the last minute?"

"Well it doesn't have to be a *real* sapphire," she scoffed, retrieving her phone. "It can be costume jewelry, no one will be able to tell. Fake ring, fake wedding. It will be fitting really."

Owen sucked in a deep breath and scratched the back of his head.

"I'll do my best," he shrugged. "What about a wedding date? We gotta do this soon."

Amy scrolled through her phone again until she reached her calendar. The most obvious date of all glared back at her and it was only a little more than a week away. It was a date that no one would question.

"It's gotta be on Valentine's Day," she said, showing him her phone. "It's only a week from now. If we are going to do a quickie wedding and not try to pull the pregnancy card, Valentine's Day is perfect."

"Pregnancy card! What the hell is…?"

Amy rolled her eyes. "People are going to assume I'm pregnant or something. If the wedding is on Valentine's Day, then it will seem romantic no matter what people think."

Owen chuckled and slapped his knee.

"Dang, Ame, you're good at this. You sure

you never wanted to get married? You're pretty good at planning a wedding."

"Oh, shut up," she said, shivering against the night. "Well, I'm definitely sober now. I should get going."

"Fine," Owen said, hopping down from the truck. He extended a hand to help Amy down. She accepted it reluctantly, trying not to think about the fact that they were holding hands again. It occurred to her in that moment that they would also be kissing again at some point.

Oh God.

"So what's the plan for tomorrow then?" she said, rubbing her arms for warmth.

"Well, I guess I'm going on a wild goose chase in the morning for a blue engagement ring," he said, shoving his hands deep into his pockets. "Then I was thinking I could pick you up for lunch with my folks and we can spring the news?"

"How do we t-tell them we g-got engaged?" she said through chattering teeth.

"I hadn't thought about that either," Owen blinked. "Man, maybe this isn't such a good idea."

"Don't worry about it," she said. "I'll th-think of something. I gotta go."

Amy reached out for a hug again, this time even more aware of his warmth and the way they fit together.

"Alright then, *fiancée*," he said, pulling away. "I'll pick you up about a quarter to twelve?"

Amy nodded.

"It's a date."

She shivered and smiled and waved good-bye, still buzzing over the unexpected proposal. Owen watched on, making sure she got in safely before stepping up into his own truck and rumbling the engine to life. Amy immediately cranked the heat in her car and waited, warming up as she watched Owen's tail lights disappear in her rear-view mirror.

Fiancée.

The sobering realization of what she had agreed to, what it all meant, and what was to come, hit Amy all in that moment. There would be pictures. Official documents. A ceremony. And most importantly, there would be at least one obligatory kiss with Owen Durant. He had barely learned to shave the last time they had kissed.

Amy tried to shake away the notion of what it was going to be like to kiss Owen again as she drove toward her parents home. It should have been no big deal; she'd kissed lots of men since that hot summer night so many years ago. It wasn't going to mean anything, right?

As Amy pulled into her parents driveway, she realized she was going to have to lie to a lot of people. Her family. Her friends. Her business associates. This wasn't just going to be a week-long or month-long affair; this was going to be something she would have to fabricate and explain for her entire life. She was going to be stuck with the notion that for a very short amount of time, she would be known as Amy Durant.

Amy moaned and leaned her head on the steering wheel of her car, surrounded by the comfort of the warm cocoon of piped-in hot air. She pictured herself and Owen, hand-in-hand in front of their family. She imagined signing official documents and saying "I do." She pictured kissing Owen, and one thought and one thought alone dominated her head and her heart for the rest of that night.

What have I done?

CHAPTER FIVE

Amy didn't get a wink of sleep that night.

While she should have been running reports and researching problems for clients, Amy instead found herself obsessively scrolling through bridal planning websites. She had scoffed at the notion of wedding planning before and considered it to be a useless waste of time. But as she scrolled past the images of illuminated mason jar centerpieces, wildflower bouquets, and smiling couples in rustic barns, something unexpected stirred inside of her.

Maybe she really *did* want to get married after all.

Nonsense, she thought, finally forcing herself to put down her phone as the clock neared 3:00 a.m. *I'm just trying to make sure this business transaction goes down without a hitch. That's all it is. An agreement between two business partners and friends.*

Regardless, Amy couldn't stop thinking about a vintage off-shoulder lace mermaid dress she had spotted on the Nordstrom website. She could see herself wearing the designer bridal gown with her hair in a low, sophisticated chignon. She would be grasping a bouquet of wildflowers gathered from the Durant property with Owen dressed in jeans and a suit jacket and his best Stetson hat. She hastily chose her size and added the dress to her shopping cart, then placed a rush shipping order. With her faux wedding dress secured and visions of rustic centerpieces dancing in her head, Amy was finally satisfied enough to fall into a restless sleep.

✿ ✿ ✿

"Rise and shine, Amy Lynn!"

The chirpy, sing-songy voice of Rhonda Grimes floated through the air and straight to Amy's ears as warm rays of sunlight assaulted her eyes.

"It's nearly eight o'clock, missy! You never sleep in this late."

"*Moooom*," she moaned. "I didn't sleep last night."

"Well, *excuuuuse* me," her mother huffed. "I thought you had work to do. Well, there's coffee and breakfast is on the stove."

Amy rolled over and glanced at the notifications on her phone. She had over thirty new emails in her inbox and a missed text message from Owen. She smiled and opened up her messages to see what Owen wanted. His text was only two words with an attached image of him holding up a round-cut purple ring. **Got it.**

She shook her head in disbelief. The stone

was an amethyst and not a sapphire, but she had to admit, it wasn't a bad dummy ring. And he had procured the prop before she was even out of bed. Maybe Owen would be up to the task of pulling this thing off after all.

That'll do, she replied. **See you soon.**

Amy considered ending the text with an emoji wink or kiss symbol for good measure, but held back. There was definitely a line when it came to this ruse and she wanted to make sure she wasn't going to cross it. She was already overly excited about planning a wedding of all things. She didn't want to allow herself to get all worked up over Owen Durant too.

Amy yawned and plodded out to the kitchen in search of sustenance, her eyes still sleepy and puffy from scrolling on her phone all night. Her mother was seated at the kitchen table with her sudoku book open and her pencil poised, a cup of black coffee in front of her. Just adjacent to the kitchen was her father, propped up on his favorite chair and tuned in to the cable news network. Even though she felt like a completely different person these days, Rhonda and Jeff Grimes never changed.

"Well, look who decided to join the livin'," her mother chided, rising from her chair. "You want a biscuit and grits to go with your eggs?"

"Just the eggs, Ma," Amy said, kissing her mother on the cheek. "Owen is going to pick me up for lunch soon."

"Oh? Seeing Owen again, huh?" she said.

"You certainly are being a good friend."

Her mother chuckled to herself as she scooped out a helping of eggs onto Amy's plate.

"*Yes*," Amy said, accepting the plate with a wry grin. "His uncle died. I'm just trying to show him some support."

"Is that what it's called these days?" Rhonda said, returning to her sudoku book.

"Oh, leave her alone, Ronnie," her father huffed from his chair. "Owen's a good boy. Him and Amy been friends a long time."

"Thanks, Dad," Amy said between hurried bites.

"You taking the day off then?" her mother asked, flipping the page of her book.

"I'm going to check my emails and take a shower. We'll see," Amy shrugged, rinsing her dish in the sink. "I've got a lot on my plate this week."

"You work too much," her mother scolded, pointing the end of her pencil in her direction.

"I know, I know," Amy said, pouring herself a fresh cup of coffee. "ViruSmart isn't gonna run itself though."

"Your ma is just teasin'. We're both real proud of ya," her father said, smiling at her from his chair. Amy leaned over and kissed him on the head.

"Thanks, Dad. Well, I better get to it."

Amy retreated back down the hall toward her room with a coffee cup in hand. She knew she should have been thinking about the security breach that almost happened with her Pets-A-Lot account or how she was going to miss out on snorkeling in Belize with Tausha. But as she entered her old room, a strange sense of nostalgia washed over her. It was getting harder and harder to push that hazy July night fifteen years ago away in her mind, and as she flopped down on her bed, she could practically smell the wet earth of the Durant farm in her nose again. She remembered all too well how awkward she felt around Owen that whole summer, obsessing about what she looked like as she prepared to head to her grandparents house for the day. After summer their brief romance fizzled, as so many teenage relationships do. Amy got a part-time job the following spring and never spent another summer with her grandparents again. She thought she might never see Owen again, but as fate would have it, they reconnected in college when they both were enrolled in the information technology program at UCF. By that time, Owen was chasing coeds, and she was chasing her dream.

Amy scrolled through her emails, deleting half of them and forwarding the other half to her assistant. She checked her wedding dress order again and was relieved to see her package was already out for delivery. Amy admitted to herself that she was going to be far too distracted to do any real work that day and hopped on wedding planning websites instead. Before she knew it, an hour had passed as she gazed upon pictures of ring bearers in suspenders and flower girls with crowns of daisies. She had never understood why people enjoyed wedding planning before, but now as she scrolled past tiered carrot cakes and gazebos lit with Edison bulbs, she was begging to see the appeal.

As Amy showered, she found herself thinking about music and first dances, reception menus, and honeymoons. There was so much to do when it came to planning a wedding and — though the prospect was of no interest to her before — as an A-type manager, the idea of putting together the perfect quickie wedding was actually invigorating. And as far as fake grooms go, she could certainly do worse than Owen Durant. Plus, there was going to be a nice payoff when it was all over. She was hesitant to admit it, but the whole prospect of planning a mock wedding to her childhood friend was actually going to be *fun*.

At a quarter to noon on the nose, Owen's black F-150 rumbled into the driveway just as he had promised. Cookie the beagle barked and howled at his arrival, prompting Jeff Grimes to say "Git!" over and over again. Amy ran her brush through her long chestnut hair and checked her reflection in the mirror one last time. She chose a cream mohair sweater and wool slacks from Etro paired with her favorite quilted Prada flats for the occasion. She wanted to look special but casual all at once, and this was the best she could do with her limited wardrobe. She grabbed her matching quilted wristlet, kissed her parents goodbye, and said a quick prayer that lunch at the Durant family estate would be smooth sailing.

Amy opened the door and nearly jumped out of her skin as Owen reached for the knocker. Cookie raced between her legs to give him a good vocal scolding, barking and whining as though a killer were at the front door. Owen kneeled down and scratched the brown and white beagle between the ears and instantly made friends.

"Hey, Old Girl," he said, scratching the dog under the chin. "It's just me."

"Owen!" Amy's mother cooed from behind. "How nice of you to stop by."

"Hey, Missus Grant," Owen said, poking his head around Amy to look into the living room. "Hey, Mister Grant."

"Hi, Owen. How's your pa?" her father shouted.

"He's good, sir. I'll tell him you asked," Owen said, tipping his hat. He looked over at Amy who was still trying to nudge the dog gently back into the house. "You ready?"

"Yeah, let's go," she said, shuffling out the door. "Bye!"

"Goodbye, kids!" Amy could hear her mother's muffled voice through the now closed front door.

"Oh my gosh, let's get out of here," she said, hurrying to Owen's passenger side door. Owen was right at her heels and ready to open it for her. "I didn't get a dang wink of sleep last night. How about you?"

"Nope," Owen said, helping her up into the lifted truck. "Not a wink."

Amy settled in and buckled her seatbelt as Owen scooted into the driver's seat. She checked her reflection in the visor mirror, making sure her hair hadn't gotten too mussed up in the fray with her mother's excited dog. When she was satisfied with her reflection, Amy slapped the visor back into place and looked over at Owen, who had a small black velvet box extended in her direction.

"I know it's not a sapphire," he said, looking down at the box sheepishly. "But it was the best I could do on short notice. It was my grandmother's."

Amy's jaw went slack as she accepted the little ring box and popped the top open. Inside was the same ring he had texted to her that morning, although in person, it was much more delicate and sweet. She removed the ring from its cushion, slipped it on the appropriate finger, and was amazed to find that it *just* fit.

"I can't have this," she said, shaking her head. "It's a family heirloom."

"Yes, you can. It's mine to give. Grandmother gave it to me ten years ago right before she passed for an occasion such as this. It would just sit in my dresser drawer otherwise."

Owen turned over the engine and his truck rumbled back to life, breaking the awkward ten-

sion between them. As he backed out of the driveway, Amy continued to examine the way the ring
looked as it glinted in the sunlight. It was a strange
notion for her to have a ring on that finger. She had
bought herself a number of fine pieces of jewelry
over the years, rings included, but had always been
careful never to wear a ring on *that* finger. She felt
silly for being so enchanted by the presence of a
piece of jewelry placed in such a symbolic, archaic
way.

"So what are we going to tell your parents?"
Amy said, finally putting her hands in her lap. "Do
we say we've been dating in secret for a while?

"I guess that'll work," he nodded, then
looked over at her with a mischievous grin. "Still
not big on the fake pregnancy idea?"

"*No*," she said sternly. "Most *definitely* not."

"All right," he said, placing a hand on his
chest. "I won't mention it again. It would make our
whole scenario seem just a little more believable,
that's all."

"N. O," she smiled, spelling it out for good
measure. "That's final."

"*Fine*. Okay, so we'll say we've been seeing
each other in secret for a while," he nodded. "You
were still enchanted with me after all these years,
and you just couldn't stay away anymore."

"No need to embellish," she said, admiring
her new ring again. "How did we get engaged?"

"Well," he said, staring at the road ahead.
"We were fishin' down at DeSoto Lake and you

caught a big one. Then I got down on one knee and asked ya."

"No," she shook her head. "I haven't been fishing in ten years. My parents would never buy it."

"*Ten years!*"

His head whipped in her direction and he nearly swerved off the road.

"But you used to fish all the time!"

"Owen, watch the road!" she scolded, hanging tight to the overhead handle. "Let's just say we got engaged at The Watering Trough when I came to visit at Thanksgiving. That's fine."

"If you say so," Owen shrugged, cutting a sharp left down State Road 247. Amy shifted uncomfortably in her seat.

"Well, we're almost there. Is there anything else I need to know?" she said, checking her reflection one last time.

Owen pulled off the road and down the familiar paved drive Amy knew so well as a child. Durant Estates was easily one of the nicest homes in the county, with a real wrought iron front gate and acres of mossy oak tree-lined front yard leading up to the hundred-year-old property. Even now as an adult, the tall columns supporting the front of his pristine white home seemed just as massive and imposing as ever.

"Oh yeah, there's one more thing," he said, pulling his truck around to their paved backyard garage. "My buddy Tucker is staying here for a while. He can get a little flirty but I'll tell him to back off."

"Noted," Amy said, opening her door. Before she knew it, Owen was already at the passenger side helping her down.

"You don't have to do that," she said, waving his hand away.

"Ame," he said, peering up at her from under his cap. "If people are going to believe that we are engaged, you're going to have to let me be a proper Southern gentleman. Just take my hand, you big baby."

"Fine," she sighed, accepting his reach. "I suppose we're going to have to get comfortable being all cozy with each other at some point."

"Right," he said, closing his passenger door. "Well, are you ready to face my folks?"

"Ready as I'll ever be," Amy said, sucking in a sharp breath of air. She smoothed the front of her slacks and tucked a wayward strand of hair behind her ear before giving Owen a reassuring smile.

"Let's go tell your parents we're engaged."

CHAPTER SIX

Amy followed Owen down the paved hibiscus-lined path past the in-ground pool to the back entrance of the estate. This was the way she had always entered the Durant family estate when she was growing up and she knew that the path led to their massive kitchen. It was the place where she and Owen would share peanut butter and jelly sandwiches and juice boxes prepared by their in-house cook, Martin. As Owen ushered her through the threshold, Amy was delighted to see Martin standing at the sink wearing his stark white apron as always.

"Martin, you remember Amy, right?" Owen said, putting his hand on the small of her back as she took in the space. The appliances were new, but the countertop and cabinets were still the same. The sun still streamed in the same way it always did around lunch time, with squares of warm yellow light dappling the wooden floor.

"Well, aren't you all grown up now? Hello Miss Amy," Martin said, extending a weathered hand in her direction. Martin had always seemed kind and soft and old as the hills when she was growing up; more of a sweet grandfatherly type than a paid employee. Amy was amazed to see him working, let alone still standing.

"Oh, 'Miss Amy' nothing. Come here," she said, waving his hand away and embracing him in a hug. He still smelled like cookies, just as she had remembered. "It's good to see you Martin."

"I was sorry to hear about your grandparents," Martin said, giving her a nod.

Amy gave Martin a weak smile and shrugged.

"Thanks, Martin," she said, glancing out the window. From the kitchen counter you could just see the roof of her grandparents old house, the place where she spent so many happy summers. Her grandparents were the only neighbors the Durant's had and she hadn't ventured to her grandparents home in years. She wondered who owned the property now.

"Is that Amy Grimes I hear?"

The sing-song voice of Debbie Durant echoed through the cavernous estate followed by the clack of expensive high heels. Owen's mother entered the room, her bright red bob playing perfectly against her green silk chiffon blouse. As usual, Mrs. Durant's flawless hair and makeup made her look camera-ready at any time of day, and despite sporting slightly sharper cheekbones and a more defined jawline, she looked exactly as Amy remembered. Amy had always been in awe of her growing up, and that admiration still held true.

"Hi, Debbie," she said, embracing Owen's mother. She still smelled the same too, she clearly hadn't switched from her signature combination fragrance of Chanel No. 5 and La Mer face cream.

"I'm very pleased you'll be joining us for lunch. We've had such an awful week, and it's just so nice to see a friendly face," she said, leading Amy toward the dining room.

Amy looked back over her shoulder at Owen who was smiling and shaking his head. She knew she was going to hear from him later about how much his mother loved her.

"Owen says that business is doing well," Debbie continued, sitting in her usual chair. "Mr. Durant and I are just so proud of what you've done with ViruSmart."

"Thank you, Debbie," Amy said, sitting at the table next to Owen's mother. She self-consciously hid her left hand in her lap, unsure of whether or not the very observant and astute Mrs. Durant had noticed her new piece of jewelry.

"Did I hear someone speak my name?"

Deacon Durant emerged, still dressed in the casual butter yellow polo and slacks he favored for golfing. Owen was the spitting image of his father, though the senior Durant man was slightly fuller in the face and considerably less sun-worn than his son.

"Hi, Mr. Durant," Amy said.

"Well, Amy," Owen's father said, giving his son a knowing grin. "How nice of you to join us."

"I'm sorry to hear about your brother," Amy offered, giving Owen a sideways glance as he took a seat next to her.

"Thank you," Owen's father said, pulling out his chair at the head of the table. "It's been a long, hard year. But we're all relieved he's now at peace."

Martin wheeled in a cart with a large silver tureen and began to ladle out bowls of butternut squash soup as a starter. Owen took out a spice shaker of cayenne and began to douse his soup in hot pepper.

"Am I late?"

A tall drink of water with a shock of blonde hair, light eyes, and a carefree gait strode into the dining room, immediately turning everyone's heads. His denim shirt was rolled to his elbows and tucked into a pair of dark denim jeans that looked to be custom-cut just for him. His eyes zeroed in on Amy and she had to quickly remind herself to close her mouth. He tipped his hat in her direction and winked before removing the wide-brimmed Stetson, causing Amy to double blink. Her cheeks were heating up and it wasn't because of the soup.

"Tucker, this is Amy Grimes," Owen said, his eyes darting to hers.

"A pleasure to meet you," Tucker said, pulling out a chair. "Are you here for the funeral?"

"Yes," Amy said, trying to avert his gaze.

"Actually, Amy's here for another reason too" Owen said, wiping his mouth with a cloth napkin.

"Owen, we don't have to," she said, her eyes darting between Mr. and Mrs. Durant and then back to Tucker.

"Amy and I are engaged," Owen said, pulling her in for a side hug.

Amy smiled weakly and displayed her left hand, fluttering her fingers to display the engagement ring. Debbie Durant squealed with joy and rose to hug Amy. Deacon Durant clapped and rose to shake Owen's hand.

"That's wonderful news!" Owen's mother exclaimed. "When?"

"Owen and I have been seeing each other for quite some time," Amy said. The words easily rolled off her tongue and tasted metallic and cheap. She fought the urge to cringe, and instantly regretted the lie that so effortlessly spilled from her mouth. "We've actually been engaged since Thanksgiving, but wanted to wait until the right time to tell everyone."

"Yeah," Owen agreed, playing along as he lowered his eyes. "We, uh. We just wanted to keep it quiet."

"Well, I'm proud of you, Son," Deacon said, slapping Owen on the back.

Tucker remained silent from across the table, his fingers steepled in front of him.

"This is just the kind of news our family needed," Debbie said, dotting the corner of her eyes with her cloth napkin. "Oh, this makes me so happy."

"That's my mother's ring I see," Deacon said, motioning to get a better look. Amy displayed it for him again. Deacon gave her a knowing look. "I think Owen's grandmother would be proud to know you have it."

"Thank you, Mr. Durant," Amy said, folding her hands back in her lap. "I know this all must seem sudden, and I do apologize for the timing."

"Don't you worry about that at all," Owen's father said, returning to his seat. "Not one little bit."

Martin brought out the salad before quickly retreating back into the kitchen. Tucker remained quiet throughout the meal and excused himself before desert. As they lunched on salmon and potatoes, Amy and Owen continued to field questions about the wedding date and other particulars regarding their future plans. Amy was amazed at how easily the lies continued to flow, how effortlessly she fabricated a whole made up relationship with Owen for the sake of his family. It occurred to her that she would have to remember all of these off-hand details and parrot them back to her own parents very soon.

"Tomorrow is the viewing for Uncle LeRoy, right?" Amy said, finally changing the subject from weddings to the impending funeral. Martin wheeled out the cart once again and served everyone coffee after clearing away the dishes.

"Yes," Owen's father said, leaning back in his chair. "The reading of the will is this evening and the viewing tomorrow. The service and interment at the Durant crypt will be on Saturday morning."

Amy shuddered at the word *crypt.* The idea of having to see Uncle LeRoy's embalmed body soon made her glad for the warm cup of coffee in her hands.

"When *were* you and Owen planning on tying the knot?" Debbie said, steering the conversation back to wedding planning. "Of course you may have the ceremony and reception here if you wish."

"Well," Amy said, clearing her voice and taking a sip of coffee. "I know it's very soon, but we were considering Valentine's Day."

"That *is* soon," his father said, nodding from across the table.

"We are going to keep it small, just family and a few friends," she assured them. She nudged Owen, who had been very silent on the matter up to now. "We want to get married in time for a Mardi Gras honeymoon, isn't that right, Babe?"

Owen shook his head. His eyelids were heavy as though he had nearly fallen asleep.

"Oh, yeah. Valentine's Day. Mardi Gras," he said, smiling weakly.

"Owen? Travelling? My, Amy, you surely are helping our son edge out of his comfort zone," Debbie said, smiling into her coffee.

With lunch nearly over, Amy excused herself to use the restroom, which she remembered was down the hall and on the right. She felt slightly buzzy and more than slightly guilty at all of the lies she had just told, though not all of them were lies. When she told his mother she had always been in love with Owen, she realized that one was probably true.

As she reached for the handle to the bathroom, the door swung wide open. Amy let out a small eek and jumped as she found herself face-to-face with a perfect complexion and a strong, square jaw.

"Oh!" she called out, putting her left hand to her chest. "Tucker, I'm so sorry."

"Nothing to be sorry about," he said. His eyes narrowed and fixed on her newly acquired ring. "Sorry for my hasty exit at lunch. Congratulations are in order."

"Oh, thank you," she said, unconsciously spinning the ring on her finger.

"Funny," he said, leaning against the bathroom door frame. "Owen and I have been friends for years. He's mentioned you, but I didn't know you were dating, let alone on the path to being engaged."

Amy pursed her lips and narrowed her own eyes. She had to pee and Tucker was blocking her way. She didn't care for the tone of his question.

"Well, *I've* been friends with Owen for over twenty years and he's never mentioned you before today," she said, tossing her hair. "If you'll excuse me, I need to use the restroom."

"No problem," Tucker said, slowly moving

out of her way. "We'll be seeing a lot of each other I suppose. I'll be staying here at the Durant estate for the next month or so while I'm having construction done on my place."

"Oh," Amy said, nodding her head as she closed the door. "Well, I look forward to getting to know you."

"Likewise," he said, smiling at her through the crack in the door.

Amy turned the lock and let out a breath she hadn't realized she had been holding. Her heart was threatening to leap right out of her chest. As Amy finished up in the bathroom, her heart continued to pound away, her thoughts a guilt-ridden blur.

He knows, she thought to herself. *He must. Why else would he look at me like that?*

Amy affixed her fake smile back in place and practiced her exit speech. She needed to get home and break the news to her parents before Debbie Durant called her mother and blew her cover. But first, she needed to have a chat with Owen on the way home. Amy returned to the dining room and hugged her future faux in-laws goodbye, silently signaling to Owen that it was time to go. Amy also said goodbye to Martin, who was taking his tea at the kitchen island. Martin gave her and Owen his congratulations on their way out. Amy wondered what else the astute personal chef had heard through the pocket dining room door over the years.

Owen was even more quiet than usual as they walked past the pool back to his truck. Amy was nearly bursting and wanted to ream him out right on the spot but saved up her scolding for the ride home. Whether Owen was simply lost in thought or could sense her bubbling anger, he certainly took his time getting back in the truck.

"What the hell was that?" she spat out as soon as he started the engine. "I thought we were supposed to make this look realistic! You were practically catatonic!"

Owen pulled out of the back parking lot, his hands gripping hard at the wheel. He stared straight ahead, his mouth a thin, tight line.

"And Tucker! What's with *that* guy? I think he's suspicious," Amy said, twirling her engagement ring again.

"You don't have to worry about Tucker," Owen said, letting out an exasperated breath. "I'll talk to him."

"So what is the big deal, then?" Amy asked, checking her reflection in the mirror again.

"I don't know, Ame," he said. "I thought I would be okay with lying, but this just feels all wrong. I'm no good at it."

"Seriously?" she said, crossing her arms. "You dragged me into this and now you're having second thoughts?"

"No," he said, shaking his head. "It just doesn't feel right."

"The damage is already done," she said flatly.

"Now we have to go do this all over again with *my* parents. Are you sure about this? Because I don't want to upset my dad for no reason. You've seen him, he's not in good shape as it is."

Owen reached a stop light and looked over at her, his face wracked with guilt.

"I'm sorry I got you into this," he said. "But you're right. It's too late to turn back now. Plus, my parents seemed really happy about it all."

"They did," Amy agreed, nodding her head. "Tucker didn't, but your mom did. She was practically planning the wedding already."

Owen laughed through his nose, his visible irritation melting a bit.

"Okay, we'll tell your folks," he said as the light turned green. "We need to make it quick, though. I have to be back for the reading of the will at four."

Amy fiddled with her ring again.

"Do you really want me to go with you to New Orleans?" Owen asked, his forehead still lined with worry. "You know I haven't been out of Lake County since college."

"It's part of the deal," Amy said, admiring her hand. "It's like your mom said. It'll be good for you to expand your horizons."

"Fine," he said, pulling into Amy's parents' driveway. Cookie spotted them from the window as Owen cut his engine. The dog was already barking and knocking the vertical blinds to and fro, announcing their arrival.

"Think you can remember everything you told my parents?"

Amy nodded.

"Okay, then," Owen said, opening his driver's side door.

"Let's get this out of the way."

CHAPTER SEVEN

"So we'll need to invite your Aunt Marlene and your Uncle Duke. Then there's your cousins, Sherrie and Mary and the twins. Oh and your father's step-sister Suzanne from High Springs, and my hairdresser, Patty...."

"I'm gonna stop you right there, Ma," Amy said, drying her hair. From the moment she and Owen announced their "engagement," Rhonda Grimes hadn't stopped gushing about wedding planning. Amy had to excuse herself and take a long, hot shower just to process everything and take a break.

"Owen and I are making our wedding small and private. Just his parents and you and dad, and probably a friend for each of us. Oh, and Owen's siblings, but that's it!" she insisted.

Her mother pouted.

"Baby, are you sure? Your dad and I never thought you would get married. And we just love Owen to bits. Don't you want to have a nice wedding?"

"It *will* be a nice wedding. Just small and intimate, that's all," she said. "I need to call Tausha and break the news to her. She's already mad at me for canceling our spring break vacation. Now I have to beg her to be my maid of honor."

"Oh, I'm sure she'll forgive you, especially when she finds out why!" her mother said, eyeing Amy's midsection suspiciously. "Are you sure there isn't something else you want to tell me? Some other reason you're rushing to get hitched?"

"I'm not pregnant, Ma," Amy rolled her eyes. "We just wanted to get married on Valentine's Day. It's more romantic that way."

"If you say so," her mother chirped. "I'm just sayin… you're getting on in years and I wouldn't mind being a grandma. Not one bit."

"Oof," Amy said, heading back to her room. "No more wedding talk for tonight. I love you, I'll see you in the morning."

"Love you too, Sweetie!" her mom called out after her.

Amy flopped into her twin bed once more and picked up her phone, dreading the call she was going to have to make to her friend. Out of everyone, Tausha would be able to see right through any of her BS. She would be the hardest to lie to of all. She closed her eyes and wondered what Owen was up to at that moment. By that time he was surely already done with the will reading. Maybe he was sitting at home with his parents, fielding the same kind of questions she was. Maybe he was out in the woods doing god knows what with Tucker.

Tucker, what a jerk, she thought to herself. *No wonder Owen never mentioned him.*

Reluctantly, Amy pulled up Tausha's number in her phone book and stared at it. She sighed and mashed the green call icon and listened as it went to voicemail. She held her breath and waited for the beep, already feeling guilty about the message she was going to have to leave. Amy wasn't normally a liar, but with every moment that passed, her fake wedding was turning her into someone she barely recognized anymore.

"Hey Tausha. It's Amy," she trilled into the phone. "Call me back when you get a minute. You're not going to believe this...."

❋ ❋ ❋

Owen kicked back in his folding chair and stared into the flames of his fire pit, a warm, half-full beer in his hand and a frown fixed on his face. His brother, Dominic, and his friend Tucker were situated in folding chairs across from him nursing their own beers. A chilly breeze blew in through the ancient oaks surrounding the Durant estate, signaling that February was just around the corner. The men sat in silence as Dominic and Tucker puffed on cigars and talked about the work they did on the Durant Ranch that day. Owen plucked away at his Fender classic acoustic guitar, the chords echoing through the acres in the cold, dark night.

"You gonna hide behind that guitar all night, or are we gonna actually talk?" Dominic said, leaning his elbows on his knees.

Owen stopped strumming and stared his brother down. Dominic was younger than him by three years, but outweighed him easily by fifty pounds. He and Dominic fought, as brothers were apt to do, but generally got along. The matter of Uncle LeRoy's will, and the convenient timing of his brother's engagement, had caused an instant and tangible rift between the brothers that the younger Durant was determined to set straight.

"What's there to talk about?" Owen said, strumming again. "You got a nice inheritance. So did Katie. You always knew Uncle LeRoy was going to leave the business to me."

"You know damn well that's not what I mean," Dominic said, inhaling a deep puff of smoke. "How in the *hell* did you get Amy Grimes to agree to marry *you*?"

"Yeah, Owen," Tucker chimed in. "When exactly did you two get together anyway?"

"Was it before or after Charity Ashwell?" Dominic chuckled.

"Or Marjorie Szykeris?" Tucker pointed out. "Wasn't that just last month?"

Owen massaged his temples as Dominic and Tucker continued to jab him across the way. He stared into the fire, trying to think.

"Well, Amy and I have a very open relation-ship," he said, lying through his teeth. "You gentle-man wouldn't be mature enough to understand that. She does her thing and I do mine."

"Whoa-ho-ho! I knew you were a liberal sumbitch, Owen, but dang. Uncle LeRoy would not approve," Dominic said, cackling to himself.

"That's all over once we're married," Owen said, sitting up in his seat. "Besides, Uncle LeRoy is long gone. He can't loom over us anymore and decide things for us."

Tucker fell quiet as he eyed Owen from across the fire. The two friends had been on the outs all afternoon, ever since the awkward lunch with Amy and his parents.

"You're awfully quiet all of a sudden," Owen said, pointing his now empty beer bottle in Tucker's direction. "Something on your mind?"

Tucker shook his head.

"Nope," he said. "When is the viewing supposed to be?"

"Tomorrow night," Owen said. "Down at St. Mary's. There's going to be a vigil and then the priest is going to say a prayer. You comin'?"

"Yup," Tucker nodded, taking a swig of beer. "Your new fiancée comin'?"

Owen nodded.

"Good," Dominic said. "I need to give Ame a good ribbin'. Owen Durant, getting married! Well I never."

Owen looked up at the heavens for answers but couldn't see a star in sight. Dark, fluffy clouds had rolled in, obscuring his view of the night sky with the promise of rain and a cold front to follow. His heart felt as dark as the clouds that hung overhead and he wondered if Amy felt the same way. He wondered what she was doing at that moment and hoped she wasn't feeling as rotten as he was. This scheme, this fake marriage… it had all seemed so easy on the surface. Now that he was knee-deep in it, he couldn't deny the sinking sensation building in his gut that this was all wrong. The sky rumbled overhead as Owen closed his eyes and wondered how long he was going to be able to keep up the charade.

How long could he keep pretending that he wasn't really in love with Amy after all?

✻ ✻ ✻

Amy swiped on a fresh coat of lipstick and sucked in a deep breath as she stared out at the facade of St. Mary's. It was nearly sunset and the waning light beamed weakly through the round rosette stained-glass window over the main front arch giving the building a magical, ancient glow. She had driven by St. Mary's a million times growing up but had never stepped foot inside the Catholic church. Her family was Episcopalian, but only on Christmas and Easter.

She patted the back of her high bun and smoothed out her black ponte shift from Anne Dummuelmeister to make sure everything was in place. Amy had considered adding a string of her mother's pearls to complete the look, but didn't want to look too cheerful. It had been a long time since she had attended a funeral and she didn't know what was customary these days. Instead, she wore only her single amethyst and wondered how many other people at the service would notice.

Owen had offered to have the rented limo pick her up with the whole family, but Amy had declined. She already felt like an intruder when it came to the Durants, though she didn't always feel that way. She had a lot of time to think about things leading up to the funeral and it occurred to her that the Durant family wouldn't be too happy with her once everything was said and done. All of the memories she was making with them now would be tainted in just a few short months, and that thought alone disappointed her and made her feel simply awful.

Nonetheless, she soldiered on and showed up as promised for Uncle LeRoy's viewing. As she walked into the cathedral, the rows of pews were already filled with over a hundred or so people that had come to pay their respects. Amy craned her head toward the front to see if she could find the members of the Durant family, but before she could locate Owen, a deep voice startled her from behind.

"Need somewhere to sit?"

Amy whipped around and set her jaw as Tucker smiled at her, his hand shoved deep into his light gray slacks. A white shirt and light blue tie made his sunny complexion glow and his icy blue gray eyes sparkle. Every blonde hair on top of his head was perfectly in place, just as perfect as his straight white teeth. He looked like a Ken doll on a spring day.

"I was looking for Owen," she said, trying not to notice how impeccably tailored his suit was. Even his ensemble was inappropriate for a funeral, it was definitely designer. "Aren't you supposed to wear black for a funeral?"

"Yeah, but all of my things are back at my house. I had to borrow this from Dominic," he shrugged.

Suddenly a low blast of organ music filled the air, signaling the start of the service.

"Shoot!" Amy exclaimed, still searching the crowd for Owen.

"Just take a seat next to me, it's okay," Tucker said, lowering himself into the last pew. "I don't bite."

Yeah right, Amy thought to herself, reluctantly scooting into the wooden pew next to him.

Amy flipped through the packet she had received at the door with a remembrance card, a prayer card, and a schedule for the service. Uncle LeRoy's weathered face stared back at her under the brim of a black cowboy hat, his expensive white porcelain veneers gleaming in the camera's flash. His bolero tie and navy suit jacket hadn't changed at all in twenty years, and Amy couldn't help but wonder how someone with so much money still could have no sense of style.

Owen had mentioned that dinner would be

served at the Durant estate after the service so Amy had saved her appetite all day. Now, as she reluctantly sat next to Tucker, her stomach began to complain. She was starving and wanted nothing more than to get far, far away from this blond cowboy himbo. She flipped through the packet to find out how long the service was going to be and her eyes bugged at the program.

"An hour and a half!" she whispered out loud, exasperated.

"Yeah, these things take a while," Tucker said, smiling over at her in a way that made her feel a little more than uncomfortable.

"Why do we need to have four songs?" she complained, making herself as small as possible.

Amy and Tucker's thighs were nearly touching in the pew, and she made the effort to hug the edge of the seat as much as possible. Tucker stretched out and made himself comfortable, resting an arm along the back of the pew directly behind her. Amy's senses heightened. Before she could protest, the priest instructed everyone to stand and sing a hymn from the prayer card. She craned her neck and continued to try and find Owen through the crowd as she mouthed the words to the song as though she knew them. Tucker seemed to keep edging closer and closer to her, and Amy didn't know if it was just because the room was packed or if Tucker had different intentions. Either way, once the song was over, Tucker behaved himself for the rest of the service. By the time the priest had said his final blessing, Amy was more anxious than ever to find Owen and report what his creepy friend was up to.

As mourners shuffled out of the church, many in cowboy hats, Amy pushed her way toward the front of the pews and finally located her friend and fake fiancé. The family was standing soberly around Uncle LeRoy's closed casket which was flanked with at least two dozen memorial wreaths and floral displays with white magnolias, carnations, and gladiolus. She could finally see all of the adult members of the Durant family from behind; Owen's younger sister Katie, his brother Dominic, and his mother and father. As she neared, Owen turned and she couldn't help but smile.

Owen had left his signature baseball cap at home and his face was clean-shaven for a change. His hair was molded perfectly in place and he looked very grown-up and smart in his tailored black suit and tie. If there weren't a closed casket behind him, Amy could almost picture that this was what he might look like on their mock wedding day. She forgot all about Tucker and his weird, almost flirty behavior as Owen smiled back at her and extended his hand. Everyone around her disappeared as she and her faux fiancé were reunited right in front of the deceased man that had brought them together.

"Amy, we didn't think you made it," he said, placing a hand at the small of her back. He gently guided her to join the rest of the family and something clicked inside. Something Amy had been repressing for fifteen years. As she stood next to Owen, surrounded by his family, nicely dressed and somberly paying his respects to his dearly departed Uncle LeRoy, Amy couldn't help but savor the moment. She breathed him in and focused on the warmth of his hand in hers. As she continued to allow herself to get lost in the feeling of that very moment, one single thought scared her and intrigued her all at once.

How long could she keep pretending that she wasn't really in love with Owen after all?

CHAPTER EIGHT

Owen followed Amy out to her car in the darkened church parking lot as a strange mixture of grief, guilt, and happiness washed over him. Being at Uncle LeRoy's funeral had made the death of his hard-to-love relative real, and even though they had their differences, all of the good memories of fishing at Lake DeSoto, learning how to ride, and talking business with his uncle, flooded back. He was glad in a way that Amy hadn't found him during the remembrance service; he didn't want her to see him cry.

Guilt also weighed heavily on his shoulders. The lies were coming easier as he told his sister and brother-in-law about his engagement. It was easy at first to tell himself that the lie would only be for a short while and it would be a means to an end. It was a good lie in some ways; with this fake marriage he would have control of the estate and the freedom to put acres and acres of Durant property to good use. But Amy. He didn't realize what this lie would do to her.

Then again, as he followed Amy to her car, he couldn't help but feel just a little better just having her at his side. Being around Amy always put him at ease and felt like the most natural thing in the world. And how the *hell* someone could look as beautiful as she did at a funeral was beyond him, but then again, that was Amy. Even as kids, when she was covered in mud from flying through the property on the back of his ATV, she was the prettiest thing he'd ever seen.

As Owen sank into the passenger seat of her compact BMW, it dawned on him how even the very vehicles they chose to drive mirrored their differences. The life she had built for herself was lightyears away from the one he wanted to live. Even though he grew up with privilege, he took it for granted and never really felt at ease in the big empty rooms of the Durant estate. Amy didn't take her status for granted. She fought for her designer clothes, luxury car, and ocean-view condo. She worked hard for what she wanted and that made her better than him. He knew it, and she probably did too. That thought alone made him realize just how far Amy Grimes was out of his league. Dominic had been right to rib him.

"So back to your folks place, right?" Amy said, backing out of St. Mary's parking lot.

"Yup," Owen said, shaking himself from his haze. "Thanks again for driving me home. I wish you had come with us in the limo, though."

"I didn't want to intrude," she said, keeping her eyes on the road.

"You wouldn't."

"There's something seriously wrong with

71

your friend Tucker," she said, glaring at him from the corner of her eye. "He kept trying to make a pass at me through the whole service."

"What?"

Owen sat up straight, fully clear now. His heart pumped hot blood to his face and his fist closed tight.

"What did he do?"

"He kept trying to get close to me the whole time," Amy said, shrugging her shoulders in disgust. "Tried to be slick and put his arm behind me on the pew."

Owen breathed heavily through his nose, seething.

"He say anything else?"

"Not really. You're right though, he's flirty alright. Will you talk to him?"

"I'll more than talk to him," Owen said, unclenching his jaw. "I'll punch him right in his dumb teeth."

"*O*," she said. "It's not that serious. If you get all full of testosterone and end up in jail that'll throw a wrench in this whole fake wedding thing."

Owen huffed again, his fist still balled up tight. Amy turned into the long drive leading up to his family estate, his ears burning. She was right. She always was.

"I know. I just don't like him taking liberties with you. Even if we weren't going to get married I would want to knock him in his teeth for coming on to you."

Amy pulled around to the back of the house and gave him a half smile, half frown. She shifted her BMW into park and cut the engine before turning to Owen. Her right eyebrow was raised high.

"Are you *jealous*?"

Adrenaline flooded Owen's legs.

Shit, he thought to himself. *She couldn't know, could she?*

"No. Why would I be jealous? You can do what you want."

Amy eyed him suspiciously.

"Good. And so can you. But I just don't want there to be a problem. I also don't want to be the reason you're on the outs with your friend."

Amy opened her car door and exited out into the night. The half moon shone down on her shoulders and Owen remembered a teenage Amy standing in that same spot all those years ago. She had a beat up old Taurus back then; her first car. It was the first summer they didn't spend together after that long ago kiss. She drove all the way over to see him after her shift at the restaurant and he couldn't give her the time of day. He was tired from an early morning session of hunting with his father and Uncle LeRoy, and his new *Call of Duty* game pulled at his attention. That's when he had lost her. He wanted to go back in time and smack his teenage self silly. He wanted to smack himself now. There was no getting around this mess he had made.

"Well, Owen, let's get through this charade,"

she sighed, following him down the darkened back path. She linked arms with him and smiled, her teeth glowing warm and bright in the dim moonlight. "Showtime."

"Yeah," Owen said, trying to ignore the tug in his heart. He enjoyed the way it felt to walk in step with her toward his warm home full of family and friends. For a brief moment, he allowed himself the fantasy that this was for real. That he and Amy were really together and that everything wasn't a lie. For just one second, he allowed himself to believe that maybe, just maybe, Amy Grimes could be in love with him, too.

* * *

"*Amieeee*! You have to tell me everything!"

Owen's sister Katie rushed the couple as they entered the Durant estate, shoving her brother aside. Katie was a carbon copy of her mother, but wore her shock of red hair in long, princess waves to her waist. As a little girl, Katie tried to tag along with her and Owen on their many adventures, but the five-year age difference often left her on the outs. Still, Amy viewed Katie as a surrogate little sister, and it felt good to be embraced by her so warmly after all this time.

"Of course, little Nicky can be your ringbearer if you want. He's only two but he can still hold a pillow. Delilah can be your flower girl, she's four and *loves* to wear fancy dresses. Oh, wait, do you even need a ring bearer and flower girl? I'm so rude."

Katie sat Amy down on a couch by the living room fireplace and a tall, ridiculously handsome man with a flawless brown complexion and movie star features plopped a chubby toddler in her lap. The baby squealed and immediately buried his face in Katie's neck.

"Hi," he said, extending a hand in Amy's direction. "Nick Jenkins. I heard you're going to be part of this crazy family too."

"I guess so," Amy said, letting out a low, nervous laugh.

For a little while, at least.

Amy blinked as the room suddenly began to spin and a stabbing pain hit her right in the gut. She suppressed a burp and took in a deep breath.

"Katie says you're in IT? Security, right?" Nick said, wrapping a protective arm around his wife.

"Yeah," Amy said, relieved to talk about something other than the wedding or the funeral. "The Durant family is my first and biggest client. Owen and I have worked together on ViruSmart for about the last seven years."

"Nick is a human rights lawyer over in Tampa," Katie said, looking up at him with big, adoring eyes. "We still live just right down the road, but he commutes there three times a week."

"Wow," Amy said. "That's so great."

"Owen and Nick have been working together to get Camp Durant off the ground. I'm just so proud of them both," she said, bouncing baby Nicky on her knee.

"I had no idea," Amy said, truly surprised. This whole time she assumed that Owen's plans for the future of the Durant family land was kinda far-fetched and half-baked.

"When will you be moving back?" Owen's sister asked. Her kind eyes and wide, genuine smile stuck a knife in Amy's heart.

"Oh, we haven't really discussed that yet," she said, searching the room for Owen. She spied him in the corner and winced. He was in a heated discussion with Tucker.

"Owen is going to make a great camp counselor. He's so great with Dominic's boys," Katie said, shifting the baby in her lap. "Have you and Owen decided whether or not you want to have kids yet?"

"I'm sorry, will you excuse me?"

Amy rose from the couch, suddenly feeling nauseous as she moved through the crowd of people. Whether it was from the heat of the room, the leftover chicken salad her mother guilted her into eating, or the stress of the past few days, suddenly Amy felt like she was going to barf. She realized she must have looked like it too as she approached Owen and Tucker, who were clearly in the middle of a very tense conversation. Their eyes opened wide as she approached them, clutching her stomach with one hand and covering her mouth with the other.

"Ame, you okay?" Owen asked, coming to her side.

"I don't feel so good," she whispered, turning her head toward the hall bathroom.

"Aw, hell," he said, jumping into action. "Excuse us!"

Owen wrapped his arm around Amy's lower back and pushed his way through the mingling crowd of his uncle's mourners. A buzz of unfamiliar faces passed by as Amy struggled to contain the contents of her stomach. Her legs felt wobbly beneath her, and Owen managed to get her to the bathroom just in the nick of time. The couple closed the door behind them as the funeral guests murmured and gossiped about the pretty bride-to-be and the deceased man's soon-to-be very wealthy nephew.

❈ ❈ ❈

"Girl, I ain't seen you ralph like that since you drank that Four Loko on graduation night."

Owen chuckled and handed Amy a washcloth as she flushed the toilet and smoothed out her skirt. She ran the washcloth under the sink and dabbed at her face, still feeling slightly dizzy, but much better.

"It must have been the chicken salad," she said, inspecting her pale complexion. "Oh god, people are really going to think I'm pregnant now."

"Good! I mean..." Owen winced as she snapped the washcloth at him. "Sorry. It'll make the urgency of our wedding a little more believable anyway, right?"

"I suppose," Amy said, leaning up against the bathroom sink. "What were you and Tucker talking about?"

The smile melted from Owen's face. He lowered his gaze to the floor.

"I told him he needs to find somewhere else to hang his hat while his house is getting renovated," he said, kicking at the tile. "Told him that he can't be hitting on my fiancée and still call himself my friend."

Amy let out a deep sigh.

"I'm sorry, O," she said, pulling him into a hug. "I don't think either of us really knew what we were getting into with all of this."

"Nope," he agreed.

"Well, I guess we should get back out there," Amy mused. "I was having a good time talking to Katie and her husband until my lunch decided to make a cameo appearance."

"Yeah, Nick is a real good guy," Owen nodded.

"I could tell," Amy said, opening the door. "It's funny to see Katie all grown up with a family. She looks really happy, though."

"I think she is," Owen agreed.

Amy looked over at her old friend, who only a few moments before had been holding her hair back as she kneeled over the porcelain throne.

Maybe we could be happy together, too, she thought to herself.

"Amy! There you are! Are you alright, sweetie?"

Debbie, interrupted her thoughts and wedged in between her and her soon-to-be faux husband. As his mother fussed and fawned over her, mourners began to exit one by one, leaving the core members of the Durant family to themselves. Tucker, as she expected, was nowhere to be seen. As the mourning party wound down for the night, Amy couldn't help but enjoy being a part of this gathering of people and wondered what her life might be like if she and Owen didn't part ways.

What would life be like if she kept the name Amy Durant for good?

CHAPTER NINE

"*Amieee*, you've got a *packaaaage*!"

Rhonda Grimes burst through the door of Amy's childhood room with a large rectangular cardboard box under her arms. It was 8:00 a.m. and Amy was already wide awake and had been propped up on her bed for the past four hours making sure to get her work done before the funeral at eleven. Now all she had left to do was to get her daily jog in around the old neighborhood, shower, and prepare herself to face the Durant family once more.

"Give it here," she said, tossing her laptop aside. The label on the box said Nordstrom, just as she expected.

"Did you order a new dress for the funeral today?" her mother asked, her forehead wrinkled with confusion.

"No, mom, something better, " she said, her heart fluttering a little. "Close your eyes."

Amy ripped open the box and sure enough, the package contained a cream lace dress. She carefully lifted the gown from the box and removed it from the plastic outer covering and displayed it at its full length.

"Okay. Open 'em."

As Amy suspected, her mother let out a squeal that would rival that of any daytime soap opera actress. Rhonda Grimes put her hands to her mouth and suppressed happy sobs as she took in the quickie wedding dress Amy had ordered in a late night fugue state only a few days before. She had almost regretted her purchase at the time, but now, as she examined the low back silk and lace mermaid gown up close, she was pleasantly surprised with her selection.

"Well, you like it, I guess?"

"Oh, Baby, I was hoping we could go down to Beaudreaux's Bridal in downtown River Ranch, but this is just lovely," she said, examining the dress. "You're going to be so beautiful."

"Thanks, Mom," Amy said, the guilt setting in again. "After the funeral we can do some more wedding planning if you want. I'm going to have to go back to Vero Beach for a few days between now and the wedding to take care of some things though."

"Oh, that's just fine. Good gracious, I still can't believe you're getting married!"

"Me neither, Ma," Amy said, staring at the dress, her heart sinking.

"Me neither."

* * *

LeRoy Durant's funeral was scheduled for

Saturday, February the seventh, at 11:00 a.m. on the coldest day that Central Florida had ever seen. Owen thought that it was only fitting that the man who had given him cause to uproot his life, the man who was so hard to get to know and love, a man that had run through six different wives before his passing, should be put to rest on the most miserable day of the year. The sun didn't cast a single ray of light and cold droplets of rain stung at the mourners' backs with a wind that howled through St. Mary's cemetery. Owen linked arms with Amy on the way to the Durant family crypt, his mood as dark as the sky overhead.

Unlike the remembrance service the night before, the internment into the crypt was at least blessedly much more brief. Four dozen or so mourners stood outside of the Durant family crypt where generations of the Durant family members had been laid to rest before. Owen's grandparents, LeRoy Durant Sr. and Ursula Durant, were still in their entombments, the space looking just as he remembered when they were laid to rest ten and eight years ago, respectively. His great grandfather, Prescott Durant, and his wife Elizabeth Durant, were also there with gravestone markings dating back to the turn of the century. Their offspring, a daughter named Dorothy who died in infancy, and another daughter, Delphine, all rounded out the occupants of the crypt. There were a dozen other plots just waiting for his mother, his father, his siblings and whatever other Durant family members may come along. The thought of being laid to rest forever in a slab next to the bones of his ancestors and relatives gave him the chills.

The priest said his final blessing and Owen's father went to speak graveside about his older brother. He told a tale of how LeRoy Durant once faced off with a Florida panther on the property when he was only twelve. He listed the achievements of the most senior member of the Durant family, from turning their modestly successful family ranching and citrus business into a global distributor of high quality beef and Florida produce. Owen watched his father tell his only living relative goodbye and felt himself choke up as a tear fell down his father's cheek. He had never seen Deacon Durant cry in his entire life, and watching his father fall apart now was almost more than he could bear.

During the entire service, Owen was acutely aware of Amy at his side and was truthfully grateful to have her there. He didn't believe in an afterlife, but if there was one, he hoped to god that LeRoy Durant was having a good laugh. LeRoy had always liked Amy when they were growing up and had often made a point to tell Owen that he did. He admired her scrappiness and followed her career from afar as she found success on her own terms. Owen knew that Uncle LeRoy would have approved of his union with Amy Grimes, if only their union was for real.

The family stood back solemnly as the funeral director instructed the groundskeepers to place Uncle LeRoy's coffin in his rightful space among the long dead Durants. The hammer clinked against the granite slab front that bore his name and date of birth and the sound echoed through the cemetery like some kind of finite bell. With one last swing of the hammer, Uncle LeRoy was sealed away for good and it was finally time to head home.

"How do you feel?"

Owen shook his head, lost in thought once again. He felt awful, but he wasn't about to tell Amy that.

"Fine. How do you feel?"

"Fine."

She answered him quickly and sealed the word with a thin lipped punctuation. She was *not* fine.

"I forgot to tell you. I ordered a wedding dress and it already came in the mail this morning," she said, exhaling deeply. "We have a lot of planning to do before we can pull this thing off."

"You did? Wow. I guess I better get myself something to wear too," Owen said, scratching his head. "Can I see what it looks like?"

"*No*," she said, emphasizing the word. "You most certainly may not. It's bad luck, you know.

"That's only if you get married for real," Owen said, his smile returning.

"I guess," she said. "We need to get a marriage license soon too. I looked it up and it takes about three days in the state of Florida."

Owen nodded and opened up the passenger side of his truck for her. He helped her up and waited for her to get settled in before closing the door gently. Amy checked her reflection as he entered the driver's seat, but she didn't need to. Despite the rain, Owen thought she still looked great.

"I'm going to have to go back home tomorrow and take care of some things," she said.

Owen nodded again and started up the truck.

"When will I see you again?" he said, backing out of the cemetery parking lot. "No pressure, just... people are going to ask, and we'll probably need to go to downtown River Ranch to apply for the marriage license is all."

"I can come on Wednesday and we can tie everything up. Valentine's Day is only a week away, so we should probably figure some things out soon," she said, staring out the window. "Everything is happening so fast."

"It really is," Owen said, keeping his eyes on the road. The rain began to pour down even faster, obscuring the country roads of River Ranch through the tinted truck windows.

"I'm glad you were here with me today," he said, gripping his steering wheel. His instinct was to reach over and squeeze Amy's hand, but he resisted the urge. He looked over at her and smiled instead. "Thanks."

"I would have done it for you fake wedding

or not," she said, looking dreamily out the window. "I like your family."

"They like you too," he said. "I think they are all convinced so far. What about your folks?"

"Oh my mother is out of her mind with happiness," Amy chuckled. "No. I don't think they suspect anything."

"Good," he said, pulling into the Durant family drive. He pulled around back to his usual parking spot, well ahead of the rest of the family. He cut the engine and sighed. It was still steadily raining outside and neither of them were eager to leave the dry safety of the truck. In that moment, Owen realized maybe he should consider parking in the eight-car garage after all.

"Well, I'm just about ready to get out of this dang suit. The after funeral lunch isn't that big of a deal. You don't have to stick around if you don't want to," he offered, giving Amy an apologetic smile.

"Are you trying to get rid of me already?" Amy said, giving him a polite jab. "No way. If I'm going to be your fake, doting wife, I have to look and act the part. I'm leaving to go home for two whole days. I need to tell everyone in that room just how much I'm going to miss my darling Owen."

"Alright, smartass," he laughed, playfully swatting at her. She grabbed his arm, and for a minute, they froze, panting and staring at each other in the enclosed front seat of his cab. His gaze trailed to her mouth and stayed there, her pink lips pulled back in a wicked, inviting smile that exposed two rows of pearly white teeth. He wanted to kiss her. God how he wanted to.

Don't do it, Durant, he scolded himself.

No amount of mourning or old, buried feelings or getting caught up in the moment would excuse him from kissing her now. She deserved better than that and he knew it. Amy had been kind enough to take the time to help him out and to go along with his crazy scheme. He couldn't repay her like *this*.

Owen cleared his throat, pulled back, and looked away, breaking the moment. He let out one more hearty laugh and shook his head, unable to look at her again. The rain was finally letting up a bit, and after a moment he finally did venture a glance her way. A strange expression crept across her face, one that he couldn't quite read. Unable to sit in the truck another moment more, Owen slapped the steering wheel and opened his driver's side door.

"Welp," he said, hopping down from his car straight into a standing puddle. "Let's get this thing over with."

CHAPTER TEN

Amy stayed at the Durant family estate all that Saturday afternoon, enjoying her time with Owen's parents and siblings until well into the night. Being an only child, and with most of her family living up north, Amy never really experienced big family gatherings or parties. She had always wondered what it would really be like to have a sibling, and her time at the Durant estate growing up had given her a little taste of that. Now as an adult, she appreciated the warm, inviting atmosphere even more. And even though she had a ton of work waiting for her on Monday and a whole list of chores to take care of back at home, there was one thought and one thought alone that dominated her mind.

Did she and Owen really just almost kiss?

Amy knew they would have to kiss at some point, but only for show in front of family or friends. The front seat of his truck during a downpour with no one else around didn't exactly qualify as a space to show off their faux relationship. For one brief moment, she thought it might happen. Owen gave her that look, and for a split second, she was sure he was going to lean in and plant one on her. She *wished* that he would. For whatever reason he pulled away from it.

That whole afternoon and into the evening as the family dined on a buffet and drank coffee, then later bourbon and scotch, Amy mulled over how she was going to bring up the topic of what nearly happened between them. She knew she would have to pull out of the agreement to get married if one or both of them were starting to catch feelings. Even if she was dead wrong about Owen's intentions in the truck, she knew she had to be honest with him about what was really in her heart. Participating in a fake wedding was bad enough, but it would be even worse if their intentions toward each other were more than platonic.

Near 10:00 p.m., Katie and her husband, Nick, threw their sleeping children over their shoulders and headed home for the night. Dominic and his two boys left as well, and shortly thereafter, Owen's mother and father retired to their wing of the estate, leaving Amy and her fake fiancé all alone in the massive great room. The fire was roaring and she had already downed three (or was it four?) glasses of scotch. The overstuffed living room sofa felt far more comfortable than she expected, and she was in no hurry to exit into the chilly February night any time soon.

Despite the fact that she was feeling very cozy, Owen sat on edge of the couch next to her with a single cushion space between them. He swirled his half-finished scotch between his hands, his elbows propped up on his knees as he stared into the fire. He had been quiet most of the evening as she gossiped with Katie, played with Owen's niece and nephews, and joked with Dominic about old times.

"Nice to be able to use the fireplace, I bet," she said, breaking the awkward silence between them. "Don't get much use for one in Florida."

"Nope, it's mostly for show," he said, finally easing into the sofa cushions. "Just like everything else around this gaudy place."

"Your house is beautiful," she said. "I've always loved it."

"It's fine, I guess."

"Can I ask a question?"

"Shoot," Owen said, taking a sip of his drink.

"Why do you still live here if you don't like it? I mean, I know your parents still live here, but this house is part of your uncle's estate, right? You're going to own it some day?"

"This place is too big for me," he said, taking another gulp. "Besides, I have a house I've been working on that I plan to live in. I'll just let Dominic or Katie have it."

Amy sat up, suddenly feeling very sober indeed.

"Wow, O. I had no idea. Where is this place you're fixing up anyway?"

Owen looked over at her and smiled.

"I don't know if you're gonna like it," he said, shrugging. "It's not like this place at all."

"*Owen*," she said, chucking a throw pillow at

him. "You've seen where I grew up. I'm not a snob about where people live."

Owen dodged the pillow and playfully tossed it back at her.

"I know, but you live in fancy condos on the beach and in the mountains now. The cozy little cottage I'm renovating isn't anything like that."

"Well, why don't you show me then? Katie was already asking me if I was going to move here after we're married. I better know where we are supposed to live as a married couple so I don't blow our cover."

"Alright," he said, finishing his drink. "Get your coat."

"What, we're going now?" she said. He held out his hand and pulled her up to a standing position. "Neither of us can drive. We practically drank that whole bottle of Johnny."

"Don't worry," he said, the dancing firelight somehow making him look even more handsome. "It's nearby."

* * *

Amy reluctantly followed Owen out into the dark February night wishing that she had worn a pair of boots instead of her thin quilted flats. It had been a long time since she had trekked through the scrub woods behind the Durant estate, but as she heard the crunch of slash pine needles beneath her feet and listened to the wind cut through the palmettos, it all started to come back to her. Those woods were sacred to her and Owen in the dog days of their youth; a vast and wild playground riddled with mosquitos and racoons and the song of the cicada. Now in the dimly lit, frozen February night, the woods took on a different kind of magic again for Amy. One filled with excitement, promise, and the feeling of adventure she had been chasing her whole adult life.

"Owen, are we going where I think we're going?" she huffed, trying to keep up with him. "You can't be serious."

"Yep, I'm serious," he called back over his shoulder. After a few more steps, the path through the woods opened up to a clearing. There, cast in pale moonlight, was the house Amy had spent so many happy summers in.

"You bought my grandparents' house?" she said, looking at him quizzically. "It must have been practically condemned. Why would you do that?"

A fresh crop of goosebumps ran up and down Amy's arms as she walked the path she had always taken from the Durant estate toward her grandparents home. The exterior had been freshly painted, a new front porch constructed, and the old brambles of bushes and vegetation that had grown up around it over the years were cut away. In truth, it was a beautiful old home, much older than the Durant estate. Her grandmother had told her that it once belonged to one of the first citrus farmers in Florida, though her grandfather would always argue that Ponce de Leon was the first to plant citrus in the south. Either way, whoever owned the grand little home had sold the citrus farming operation to the Durants' under the condition that they could keep their homestead. The Durant family ended up owning the property in the end just the same.

"Do you want to go inside and look around?" Owen asked, taking a huge bundle of keys from his pocket. "The plumbing is still a little iffy, but I've got the electric all worked out."

Amy nodded and followed him silently up the porch and into the other house she had called home in her youth. The screened front door slapped on loose hinges against the side of the house, and with some effort, Owen was able to push the heavy old door open into her grandparents' living room.

"The second floor still needs some work, but I've been able to restore pretty much everything on the first floor. The kitchen is a little more modern than you'll remember but that couldn't be helped."

Amy walked slowly through the front sitting room, standing in the space where her grandfather's favorite chair used to be. Directly across from that was the spot where her grandmother used to sit and read with the windows open when the humidity wasn't too bad. She ran her hands along the freshly painted wainscoting and looked up at the newly installed light fixtures overhead.

"You've done a really good job," she said.

"Thanks," he said, his hands shoved deep into his pockets. "This place is all a part of the plan for Camp Durant. I'm going to run my office out of the back sunroom that overlooks the clearing."

"That was always my favorite room, too," she said, hugging herself.

Owen was still standing guard by the front door with his arms folded in front of him as she wandered through the house. When she was satisfied with her inspection, Amy rejoined him near the entrance, smiling.

"Owen, we have to talk about what happened in the truck," she said, mirroring his stance. "Did you want to kiss me?"

"What? No," he scoffed, throwing his hands up in confusion. She could always tell when he was lying. Owen was terrible at overacting.

"Not even just a little bit? Not just out of curiosity?" Amy said. "I mean, don't you think we should practice anyway? It's going to look awkward as hell if we have our first kiss in front of everyone at the wedding and flub it up."

"Psh, you're drunk," he said, exiting the house into the dark of night.

"*You're* drunk!" she called out after him, her voice echoing through the clearing. "Owen, I'm being serious! People will know something's up if we look awkward together."

Amy's heart pounded in her chest as she followed him out of the house. He closed the front door to her grandparents' home — now his home

— and bolted the lock.

"I've kissed plenty of women. I don't need to practice," he sniffed, stuffing the keys back in his pocket.

"Yeah, and I've kissed plenty of men and I can tell you right now, none of you are the same," Amy said, her hand placed defiantly on her hips.

"Well, we already kissed once. Or did you forget?" he said, brushing past her. He was walking fast through the clearing back toward the estate.

Amy let out a snort of disgust and followed at his heels through the trees.

"That didn't count and you know it. I didn't know what I was doing back then, and neither did you!"

"Speak for yourself!" he laughed over his shoulder, picking up his pace now.

Amy shivered and moved faster to try and keep up with him.

"Hey, slow down!"

Owen halted to a stop under the pine scrub canopy, catching her off guard. Amy held up her forearms just in time to keep from crashing face-first into his chest.

"Alright then, Miss Big City Amy Grimes. I'll give you a practice kiss, but only under one condition."

Owen held her by the forearms, their bodies the only warm things in the wintry, dark forest. She shivered under his touch, their breath puffing into vapor just inches away from each other's face.

"Shoot," she said.

"Condition number one: I can't kiss you and you can't kiss me if we secretly love each other."

Amy smiled and nodded.

"Condition number two: I can't kiss you if you're drunk."

Amy shook her head. She was stone cold sober by now.

"Condition number three: If I kiss you and you feel some kinda way afterward, we *can't* get married even for fake, and you *better* tell me the truth."

Amy laughed.

"That's three conditions."

Owen held her tighter, their eyes locked in that almost moonless night.

"Alright then, you asked for it."

Amy closed her eyes and tipped her face up toward him, an expectant smile spread across her lips. She was a big girl. She could take a kiss from Owen Durant and survive to tell the tale. This was just the icebreaker they needed. What was the harm?

Owen placed one hand on her shoulder and cradled her chin toward him with the other. She opened her eyes and before she knew it his lips were on hers, and it didn't take long for her to realise that his kiss was *nothing* like it was fifteen years ago. Firmly, and somehow gently all at the same time, he kissed her good and deep and long on the same patch of dirt they both used to scamper across so many years before. He kissed her and he kissed her and he kissed her until both of them were breathless and Amy finally had to pull away.

"There now. You satisfied?" Owen smiled.

Amy blinked, and for once didn't have a retort to sling back at him.

She *was* satisfied.

And that was going to be a big, big problem.

CHAPTER ELEVEN

Amy packed her things early the next morning, her thoughts still scrambled from the unexpected and better-than-good kiss Owen Durant had laid on her the night before. To be fair, she had asked for it, but she thought she could take it. Amy Grimes, independent business woman, solemnly sworn to be single and free all of her days, was getting married soon to a man that she probably, no, *most definitely,* loved.

As she stuffed the last five days' worth of dirty laundry into her duffle, Amy mulled over her choices. She knew what the right thing to do was. She should just come clean and tell Owen how she felt and then call the wedding off. But the money. The *money*! She couldn't leave a half a million dollars on the table. And she definitely couldn't let Owen down, especially since their fake marriage was the one thing standing between him and his dreams. After a long, hard run and an even longer crying session in the shower, Amy decided she could suck it up just a little while longer.

Besides, I'll be back home in Vero Beach for a couple of days, she reasoned with herself. *I won't have to see him that much until the wedding.*

She laughed to herself and remembered their embrace from the night before. Owen just casually walked it off like it was no big deal, but she was reeling from the inside. Obviously, he didn't feel like she did or else he would have told her right then and there. The worst thing about the whole situation was that she had absolutely no one to talk to about it. She considered telling Tash, but then she knew her very best girlfriend would probably not agree to be her maid of honor, and rightly so. *More lying.* Amy sighed at the prospect.

After a late breakfast of her father's famous Belgian waffles, Amy kissed her parents goodbye and promised to be back in a few days. She conveniently left out the part about visiting her grandparents' home and the fact that Owen was renovating it. She didn't know how her father would take that news, though it seemed likely he may already know. Of all the people that Amy hated lying to, she regretted having to lie to her parents the most. Though deep down, way deep down, there was still a small part of her that hoped their nuptials would stick after all.

Amy continued to shake off the notion of moving back to River Ranch for good as Owen's wife as she sped back across I-4 toward home. A little time spent back in her old routine would likely cure her of any silly notions of suddenly becoming someone she didn't really want to be. She assured herself that the wedding would come and go in no time at all, and soon she would be back to life as normal. It was going to be hard for her to keep this sort of thing a secret forever, but Amy reasoned with herself that it would be even harder to pass up a big windfall of cash.

As she pulled into the parking garage at her condo three hours later, her phone pinged with Tausha's familiar Beyoncé ringtone. Amy smiled and answered.

"Hey, Tash," she said, looking out toward the blue Atlantic waters again.

"Wanna meet up for dinner tonight? There's something I have to ask you."

* * *

Amy stepped out of her car and handed her keys to the valet at Portico, the tapas and wine bar that she and Tausha usually defaulted to. It was the kind of bottle service, V.I.P. club she was usually drawn to where the men had a dress code and dinners were paid with black Amex cards. The kind of place Amy used to like to be seen in, but as she stepped into the darkened, velvet-walled entryway of the exclusive club, she couldn't help but think that she would rather be at The Watering Trough instead.

Tausha had been the one true friend that Amy had made in college in the IT program besides

Owen. As the owner and operator of an online security business, Amy rarely got face time with most of her coworkers and clients that lived all around the world, and as a result, she hadn't made many new connections as an adult. She was extra grateful for Tausha's friendship and their love of fashion and the finer things in life. Their shared knowledge of all things IT made their bond virtually unbreakable.

As a result of living together, Tausha knew Amy better than just about anybody. Amy knew Tash could always tell when something was wrong or when she wasn't feeling well. So when she sidled up to the wine bar next to her waiting girlfriend, Amy already suspected that her friend knew something was wrong. Tausha had dressed up for the occasion in a mauve satin jumpsuit and heels, wearing a massive pair of collarbone-grazing hoops with her locks piled high on top of her head. The two friends greeted each other with hugs and Amy ordered a bottle of 2011 Mailly L'Intemporelle Rose Grand Cru for them to share.

"Pink champagne?" Tausha said, her voice raised an octave. "What are we celebrating? Certainly not our trip to Belize, which I'm still a little pissed about, by the way."

Amy sat up straight, her lips pursed together in a thin line. She knew Tausha wouldn't buy any kind of lie or story she told her about Owen or her impending wedding.

"Owen and I are getting married."

The bartender brought their frosty pink bottle of champagne out at just that moment and popped the cork. Amy extended her left hand to show off the engagement ring as proof. Tausha's mouth hung open in an "O" of surprise as their champagne flutes were filled. Amy smiled and picked up a glass and handed it to a gobsmacked Tausha, then picked up a glass for herself.

"Well, aren't you going to congratulate me?"

"You are marrying *Owen*? Owen Durant?" Tausha said, throwing back her expensive champagne. "Our rich client from Durant Farms? The same Owen Durant we went to college with? *That* one?"

"Yup," Amy said, draining her own glass.

"What happened at that funeral?" Tash laughed, shaking her head. "I didn't even know you were dating. How could you hold out on me like that?"

"We weren't dating," Amy admitted. "We just got engaged this weekend."

"I am so confused," Tausha said, pouring herself another glass of champagne.

"That makes two of us," Amy said, her eyes darting around the room. "Tash, I have to tell you something and you have to promise to keep it a secret."

The word secret immediately got her attention. Tausha leaned in.

"What is it, girl?" she whispered. "Are you pregnant?"

"No! Why does everyone immediately think that?" Amy said, pouring herself another glass of champagne.

"Well then what is it?" Tausha said, slapping the bar top. "Don't leave me in suspense."

"His Uncle LeRoy put a clause in his will before he died that stated Owen had to be married to get his inheritance," Amy said, biting her lip.

"That is the dumbest thing I heard in my whole life," Tasha said into her champagne flute.

"So he asked you to marry him?"

"Yep."

"Is he gonna pay you?"

"Yep."

"That is still the dumbest thing I have ever heard," Tausha said, tsking and shaking her head.

"You have to keep this a secret, Tash. I need you to be my maid of honor and I knew that if I didn't tell you the truth you would just figure it out anyway."

"Your maid of honor? When is this fake wedding supposed to happen?" Tausha said, flustered.

"This Saturday."

"On *Valentine's Day*? Oh no, I can't. Miguel already got a babysitter and we got a hotel, do you understand what I mean? I love you girl, but I'm not giving up a night off for your fake wedding."

Amy heaved a sigh of relief.

"Oh, thank god," she said, draining her second glass. "We are going to get the marriage annulled after all of his inheritance is transferred anyway."

"Good, I guess," Tausha said, her eyebrows arched high.

"Thank you for being so cool about all this."

"Well, I didn't say I liked it," Tausha said, smiling softly now at her friend. "But I promise I won't say a word."

Amy spun the ring around her finger, a habit she had gotten into since it was placed there only a few days ago. In any other circumstance she would have wanted her best friend to be at her side during her wedding, but in this case, it would be better if she wasn't there.

"There's something else, isn't there?" Tausha asked. She leaned on the bar with her elbow and rested her chin on her hand.

Amy nodded.

"You really like him don't you?"

Amy nodded again.

"So what are you going to do, girl? You can't get married to someone for fake that you like for real!"

"Don't I know it," Amy said, as a buzzing sensation caught her attention. She fished her phone out of her clutch. There was a single message from Owen. His ears must have been burning.

Justice of the peace booked for 10 am Saturday. Should I get myself a ring and a suit?

Amy stared at the phone for a moment and then back at her friend.

"Tash, what should I do?"

✳ ✳ ✳

Owen tossed his phone into his duffle bag and zipped his camo gilly suit all the way up. It was freezing out and he still had a lot of planning to do before the wedding on Saturday, but Dominic insisted on one last hog hunt as a bachelor party of sorts. It wasn't that he minded going on a hog hunt with his brother, hell, it was one of his favorite things to do. But his head and his heart were pre-occupied with one thing.

He was stupid in love with Amy Grimes.

In less than a week, they would come together in front of their families and tell the biggest lie either of them had probably ever told, and for what? Well, Owen knew what it was for. Money was always as good a reason as any to lie, right? But the more Owen thought about the plan, and the closer he got to Amy, the more he doubted whether he really wanted to go through with the whole thing after all.

That *kiss*. It was the kiss that did him in.

He could blame the moonlight or the way Amy's hair smelled or the breeze rustling through the pines, but the truth was, it was his own ego that got him in trouble. Owen Durant, the ladies man of River Ranch, could handle kissing a girl, especially one that practically felt like his own sister. Except Amy didn't feel like his sister. Maybe she never really did.

"You comin' or what?"

Dominic hopped on his ATV and brought the four-wheeler to life, the smell of gasoline and the crunch of machinery snapping Owen out of his Amy-induced haze. He hopped on his Raptor, parked right next to his brothers, and secured his helmet before his own ATV roared to life. He looked over at Dominic, his teeth glowing in the dark.

"What are you smiling at, dumbass?" he yelled to his brother over the dueling motors.

"You!" Dominic shouted back to him. "I ain't never seen you like this."

Owen shrugged.

"It's just nerves," Dominic assured him. "It'll pass."

Dominic revved his engine and sped off down the trail toward their hunting encampment, leaving Owen in the dust.

"I'm in love with Amy!" he called out over the roar of the engines. A weight lifted off of his chest as he announced it to the world, even if no one heard him.

Owen threw his ATV into gear and tore off after his brother, his confession lost to the wind, still known only to him.

CHAPTER TWELVE

The day of the Grimes-Durant wedding was fast approaching and both the bride and groom were holding fast to their ends of the bargain. Amy had spent two whole days back home in Vero Beach tying up loose-ends at work, taking care of chores at home, and trying her hardest not to think about how she actually loved Owen.

With a little guidance from his mother, Owen had ordered a small reception dinner and a cake for twelve, hired a photographer, secured a justice of the peace, and even got himself a ring and rented tux. All in all, he was pretty impressed with his own quickie wedding planning abilities. When Amy was set to arrive Wednesday afternoon, all they would have to do was apply for their marriage license and they would be ready to wed.

Much to Amy's chagrin, Owen's mother, sister, and her own mother had all conspired together to throw her a combination bridal shower/ bachelorette party the night before the wedding. Amy wanted to avoid parties or gift-giving of any kind, simply because she knew that in a short amount of time, they were going to have to give them back. But there was no stopping the force that was Debbie Durant and Rhonda Grimes when it came to party planning.

Amy blew back into River Ranch at just after 3:00 p.m. on Wednesday, still fully in denial of her emotions. Owen was already waiting for her outside the Lake County courthouse, leaning up against his truck and wearing his usual uniform of tattered baseball cap, jeans, and a long-sleeve tee. Amy wore her favorite puff-sleeve polka dot dress from Dries Van Noten for the occasion, and shook her head when she regarded Owen's casual ensemble.

"I should have known better than to dress up," she said, greeting him with a smile as she got out of her car.

Owen looked down at his work boots and jeans.

"Should I have worn something nicer? I got a tux for Saturday," he said, defensively.

"No, you look fine. You look great," she said, staring at the ground more than at him.

"This is your last chance to back out," he said, looking up at the courthouse. "You still wanna do this?"

Amy looked at him and shook her head. She thought of her condo in Colorado and what it would be like to have it paid off. She thought about all of the kids that would stomp through the woods behind the Durant estate, enjoying their summers just as she and Owen had. She thought about Uncle LeRoy, probably laughing down on them.

"I do," she nodded. "I mean I will. I will say I do. I mean… let's go get this over with."

Owen laughed through his nose and followed her into the courthouse, her black patent pumps clacking on the sidewalk in front of him.

"When this is finished I'm going to have to get us matching T-shirts that say 'Let's Get This Over With.'"

She looked over her shoulder and shot him a dirty look as she gripped the courthouse door handle. Amy finally looked Owen in the eye for the first time since their practice kiss on that chilly night not so long ago.

"Are we still going to be friends after all this?" she asked, still pausing at the front door.

"I don't see why not," Owen said. "Amy, you're always going to be my best friend."

Amy smiled and let out a sigh of relief.

"Good. Now let's get in there and pretend to be in love."

* * *

After paying the courthouse fees, Amy and Owen escaped into the late February afternoon with a marriage license in hand. They were one step closer to being legally wed and they walked out to their respective vehicles in silence. The sun was hovering just above the horizon, meaning that they only had two more full days to get everything in order. Amy leaned up against her car, shivering in her thin dress and wishing she had brought a coat.

"I booked a hotel for our honeymoon, right on Bourbon Street. We'll be able to watch the Mardi Gras parade from our balcony," Amy said.

"Oh yeah," Owen said, sucking in a deep breath. "I almost forgot about that."

"You agreed!" she reminded him. "I already had to give up snorkeling for this. I'm not going to miss out on New Orleans too."

"It's just that travelling makes me nervous. I get all edgy if I have to be in a car or a plane for too long."

Owen shoved his hands in his pockets and leaned up against his truck.

"Well, it's only an hour drive to Tampa, and then less than two hours on the plane," she said, giving him a half frown. "It really bothers you that much?"

"Yeah," he said, kicking at a pebble. "I tried to get on a plane to head out to Vegas for Dominic's bachelor party and ended up having a panic attack in the airport."

"*No*," she said, her eyes growing wide. "You never told me about that."

"Well, it's embarrassin'," he admitted.

"I'll be right there with you," she reassured

him. "We'll both have a couple of scotches in the bar airport and it won't be so bad. You'll see."

"I just don't want you to get upset with me if I freeze up at the airport," he said, jangling his keys. "You're so used to it all. I feel bad if I would be holding you back."

"You wouldn't," Amy said, and walked his way. She leaned up on his truck next to him. "Sometimes you just need someone to help you get over your fears. Like when I fell out of that tree. You didn't let me stop climbing trees right? You made me get up there and try again."

"Yeah, but you were a kid. I'm a grown-ass man. I should be able to go somewhere new and not freak out."

"There is no *should.* We're not robots. We're all built differently," she said, placing a reassuring hand on his shoulder. He looked down at her hand and she pulled it away as though she had touched fire.

"I don't know about you, but I'm sick of all this wedding talk," she said, changing the subject. "What's there to do in River Ranch these days instead of shoot at things and get drunk?"

Owen looked down at her, crossed his arms, and snorted.

"I have a few ideas."

* * *

"I should have known. Oh no. *Hell* no."

Amy stared daggers at Owen as he handed her a helmet and removed the dustproof covers from his ATV.

"Why not? I'm gonna drive. All you gotta do is hang on."

"First of all, it's dark and totally dangerous," she said, her lower lip poking out in disapproval.

"I ride around back here in the dark all the time. There's only a few potholes and they're small," he said, throwing her a wicked smile.

"Second of all, this is a $600 silk dress and I am wearing heels," she said, shaking her head.

"Well, you're gonna have a cool half million this time next month," he said, snapping the helmet on his head. "You can buy a dozen new dresses."

"How can you ride around on this death trap but be too scared to fly?" she asked, reluctantly fitting the helmet to her head.

"Because," he said, swinging his leg over the four-wheeler. "It's my land and my machine. I'm in control."

"Oh my god," she said, gingerly scooting into the seat behind him. "Okay, but just one lap or something."

"We'll see," he said, revving the engine.

Amy's breath caught in her throat and she instinctively wrapped her arms around Owen's waist. She was wearing a dress and straddling him from behind and the whole situation felt completely inappropriate. She loved it just the same.

"After one loop, you'll be begging me for more!" he shouted over the rumble of the engine. "You ready?"

"I guess!" she shouted into his ear.

"Alright then let's go!"

Amy's head snapped back as the ATV lurched forward into the night down a hollowed out path through the woods. Owen had lied; there were *tons* of potholes and the ATV seemed to catch every one, bouncing them up and down along the path. Despite the frigid February wind stinging her cheeks and the fear of falling off constantly at the back of her mind, Amy felt herself letting go and enjoying the dark, sweet smelling woods as they whizzed by. In truth, she just enjoyed leaning into Owen's back and being close to him.

By the time they had circled back to the massive garage outside of the Durant estate, Amy's cheeks were chapped and her hair was matted to oblivion. The rumble of the ATV engine had left her ass feeling numb, but otherwise she felt exhilarated, and just a little bit closer to Owen than before.

"Okay Durant," she said, taking off her helmet. "You got me. I guess I can see the appeal."

"It's fun, right?" he laughed, beaming back at her. "You wanna go again?"

"No, I need to get to my folks' house," she said. "I have an appointment with a tailor tomorrow morning to get my dress taken in, and then I have to find a local hairstylist."

"Aw, more wedding talk," he said, cutting his engine.

"What!" she said, exasperated. "If this is going to look legit then I need to act like I care!"

"No, I appreciate all of your effort," he nodded. "I'm just teasing you."

"Your mom and sister have a little thing planned for me Friday, so I'll probably see you then," she said. "What are you up to until then?"

"Oh, just doing some work for Durant. I have a meeting with my lawyer about setting up the foundation. It's going to take a long time to get things off the ground. I really can never repay you for helping me do this to move everything forward."

"You could make it a million dollars instead?" she teased, kicking a little dirt his way.

"Nice try," he said. "I'll make it seven-fifty if I don't have to get on a plane."

Amy pondered for a moment and then shook her head.

"No deal, you're going on a vacation with me," she said.

They both stared at their feet. The warmth of Owen's body against hers was beginning to wear off and Amy shivered as the chill of night set in.

"Well, I guess I'll see you Friday, and then it's the big day," she said, looking over at him expectantly. Her rational side knew that she should just get in her car and go home. Her good sense told her that she should just suck it up for two more days and finish this whole thing so she and Owen could collect and go back to their normal lives. But her irrational side… her irrational side wanted to ask for another practice kiss and then maybe a little bit more. Her irrational side said half a million dollars be damned.

"You better get going before you catch your death out here," he said, a puff of vapor escaping from his lips.

"We could go in and get warm by the fire?" she ventured.

Owen shoved his hands deeper in his pockets and thumbed his nose.

"You wanna go sit by the fire pit with me?" he asked.

"Why not?" she shrugged.

"Thought your parents were going to be up waiting for you," he smiled.

"They'll understand," she said. "I'll just tell them I'm with my fiancé."

Owen looked back at her and ran his fingers along his jawline as if in thought. She couldn't quite tell in the dark, but his smile almost looked a little sad.

"Alright," he finally said. "If you ain't still worried about messin' up your fancy dress, come help me get some firewood."

With that, Owen disappeared into the dark with Amy trailing right behind.

CHAPTER THIRTEEN

"I've been trying to tell my dad and Uncle LeRoy forever that they don't need me to run the IT side of the business anymore."

Owen swigged from a bottle of Apple Jack before passing it to the left. Amy accepted the too-sweet liquor and put her lips to the bottle, wincing as the fire hit the back of her throat.

"Ugh," she shuddered. "I almost forgot how bad this stuff was."

Amy passed the bottle back to him and stared at the fire. It was still chilly out, but between the roaring fire pit and the shared bottle of apple-flavored whiskey, Amy wasn't minding so much anymore.

"So why don't they let you outsource your IT operations? I don't see what the big deal is. ViruSmart can work with whoever you pick to run things," she said.

"Dad thinks it's just an excuse for me to stomp off in the woods all day. I think he's the one that got in Uncle LeRoy's ear, if you ask me."

"I'm sorry," Amy pouted, starting to feel the effects of the alcohol. "I thought things were good between you and your folks."

"They *are* good," he said, nodding. "But they don't understand me. Mom and Dad are more at home at the golf course club or on the greens. Plus I went to school and got my degree and they think I should use it, I guess."

"But what about Dominic? He works on the ranch doesn't he?"

"It's different with Dom. I'm the oldest and I finished school. I'm the eldest Durant so it's all up to me."

Owen passed the bottle back to Amy. Her eyelids were getting heavy, but she didn't feel like moving. Owen was finally opening up to her and talking about things he never mentioned in twenty years of friendship. She wasn't about to leave while he was freely shooting off his mouth. Whether it was the Apple Jack or the stress of the impending wedding, Owen was extra chatty, and Amy just drunk enough to take advantage.

"Owen, why didn't we ever date in college?" she asked, passing the bottle back to him. His gaze caught hers; two dark pools flickering in the firelight. He took another sip before opening his mouth again.

"Well, I didn't know that you wanted to."

Owen sat up straight in his chair and offered the bottle back to Amy. She waved it away.

"Course I did, you dummy," she said, and

yawned. "Why do you think I followed you around like a lost puppy every summer?"

Owen snorted.

"I just thought it was because you lived so close," he said, taking another sip.

Amy closed her eyes and laughed as she burrowed down into her camp chair.

"You were such a hotshot in college. I had to work twice as hard as you did. Coding and programming," she yawned. "All of that came so naturally to you. I was always working or studying anyway, I guess."

"I gotta stop giving you brown liquor," he laughed, shaking his head.

"Mhmm," she said, her breath coming in slow and shallow.

Owen waited another moment longer until a soft whirring noise emanated from her nostrils.

"If I knew you wanted me, that would have been it, and we wouldn't be here right now. I would have asked you to marry me a long time ago, and for real."

Amy didn't answer and continued to saw logs as Owen stared into the fire.

Two days. He only had two days to fix this or finish it, and for the life of him, Owen couldn't figure out what to do.

"Come on, drunky," he said, lifting her from her camp chair. He lifted her like a baby and wrapped her limp arms around his neck, just like a groom bringing a bride across the threshold. A very inebriated bride.

"Noooo," she murmured in her sleep. "I don't wanna get married."

Owen stopped in his tracks and looked down at a still sleeping Amy, soft and vulnerable in his arms. She didn't want to marry him. She said so. And even though he wanted nothing more at that moment than to kiss her she had given him all of the answers he needed.

"Let's get you settled on the couch," he sighed, trekking toward the back entrance to Durant Estates.

Martin will make her scrambled eggs and coffee in the morning and she would forget everything they said, he reasoned with himself. *We both will.*

Owen placed her on the giant sectional sofa in their great room and covered her with a blanket. He kissed her on the forehead and removed her high heels, placing them by the fireplace right next to his work boots. Owen laid down on the opposite end of the sofa and stared at the ceiling for what felt like hours that night, willing for the night to bring him a few blissful hours of mindless sleep.

❊ ❊ ❊

She thinks my tractor's sexy!

Owen shot up straight, his heart racing as his eyes darted around the great room. He rubbed his eyes and grabbed his phone from the coffee table, just barely missing a call from Amy. The time on his phone said it was well past 9:00 a.m. and the spot where he had left her on the couch the night before was empty.

I still need to change that damn ringtone, he grumbled to himself.

With a throbbing head, Owen stood up and struggled to remember what happened the night before. He shuffled to the kitchen where he promptly downed three ibuprofen chased with a half cup of black coffee. The stress of the wedding was driving him to drink more than usual and he was paying for it. Once he had finally cleared his head enough, Owen checked his phone again to see that Amy had left a message. He put the phone to his ear and listened to Amy's cheerful, clearly-not-a-hungover-as-his voice sang in his ear.

"Hey, it's Amy, I'm going to get my wedding gown altered today and I'm going to try to book a hairdresser for Saturday. Oh, and I'm going to order a bouquet with a boutonniere to match for you. Let me know if there are any flowers you are allergic to or that you just hate. I'll probably be busy most of the day so we'll catch back up tomorrow? Okay, bye."

"Well, good morning."

Debbie Durant swooped in behind her son in a flurry of peach sateen and houndstooth. Her hair and makeup were flawless, as usual.

"Mornin'."

"We have an appointment to pick up your suit at 10:00 a.m. Will you be ready by then?"

He massaged the space between his eyes and

sipped his coffee.

"Yeah, I just need to get a quick shower and we can go, I guess."

"Owen," she said, leaning against the counter. "You know we're all fond of Amy."

"Not this again," he groaned. "I told you already, I'm fine. Everything is fine."

"It just seems like you're a little hesitant about this whole thing," she said, placing a reassuring hand on his back. "I'm just saying no one will be upset if you want to delay the wedding. We could put on such a lovely wedding for you both in the summer instead."

"It's not that... it's complicated."

"You have a lot on your plate, and lord knows LeRoy didn't make things easier for your father and I. We just don't want you to rush into something unnecessarily. Do you understand what I'm saying?"

Owen sipped his coffee again and looked over at his mother. Their relationship hadn't always been the easiest, but he never doubted whether or not she loved him. Though Debbie Durant could be abrasive when it came to business, when it came to matters of the heart, she was just as soft inside as he was.

"Mom, I love Amy," he said.

"I know sweetie. I'm glad."

Owen clenched his jaw. The words were on the tip of his tongue. He could just admit everything to his mother right now and then maybe he could figure something out. Instead, Owen finished his coffee in silence, frozen by his indecision.

"I'll be fine," he said, looking at the lock screen on his phone. A smiling photo of Amy stared back at him.

"Let's go get my tux."

❊ ❊ ❊

"It's practically perfect."

Rhonda Grimes stood back, admiring the cream lace mermaid gown her daughter had chosen for her nuptials just a few days before. Amy regarded her reflection and had to admit; she was right. For a gown that was quite literally chosen off the rack and on a whim, the long-sleeve, backless number seemed to fit her like a glove.

"So long as you don't lose or gain an ounce in the next two days, I'd say you're good to go."

Her mother's good friend and go-to seamstress, LuAnne, pulled a straight pin from her mouth and secured the last inch of hemline on the gown.

"I can have this sewed up for you today and you can pick it up tomorrow."

"You're an angel, Lu," Amy said, hugging her mother's friend.

"You know, Ronnie didn't even tell me you were getting married! I was so surprised, but I'm more than happy to bump my other clients for you," LuAnne said, smiling at her handiwork.

"Yes, I think we surprised a lot of people," Amy said, looking out the window. Downtown River Ranch was bustling for a Thursday morning in February, and as LuAnne put her final touches on the dress, Amy stared out the storefront window in wonder. Young mothers pushed babies in strollers down the sidewalk with steaming cups of cocoa, retirees walked their dogs along the lake across the way, cars continually drove by down Main Street. River Ranch had almost completely changed its whole atmosphere since she ran away from it all more than a decade ago.

"Downtown seems kinda hip these days," she said, looking at her mother incredulously.

"Yes, there's a lot more going on in town these days," her mother agreed. "You used to complain every day in high school how boring River Ranch was and how you couldn't wait to get away. Maybe if they had just installed a Starbucks on the corner back then you wouldn't have wandered so far off."

Amy frowned. Her mother didn't guilt her often on her lifestyle, but when she did, it hurt. Changing the subject was in order.

"Tausha said she couldn't make it. We're going to have Owen's niece and nephew serve as flower girl and ring bearer, but I'm going to be without a maid of honor."

"Oh, what about Owen? Didn't he have a best man?"

"I think his friend Tucker was supposed to

stand in, but they're not speaking at the moment," Amy said, picking her nails.

"Your father is so pleased he'll be able to give you away," her mother said, her voice cracking.

"Oh, Ronnie."

LuAnne left her hemming job and went to her friend's side. Amy blinked, frozen as she watched her mother try to compose herself.

"Oh, don't fuss over me, I'll be fine," she said, swatting her friend away. "It's just, we don't know how much time he has with us. It will be good for him to do this one traditional thing for you as a father and daughter. It will do him some good."

Amy swallowed hard. Any inclination that she had of playing runaway bride in that moment was now officially out the window.

"I think I need to step out of this dress," she said, fanning herself. "Lu, are you just about done?"

"Sure, Sugar," LuAnne said, helping her down from her box stand. "And congratulations. You're going to make a truly beautiful bride."

"Thanks, Lu," she said, regarding her reflection in the mirror again.

A beautiful liar is more like it.

Amy gathered her fitted lace mermaid skirt and carefully edged back into LuAnne's tiny changing room. Whether it was from her father's Belgian waffles or a stifling sense of anxiety and guilt, the dress seemed to constrict her, making it hard for her to breathe. Beautiful as her ill-begotten dress was, she couldn't stand to wear it a moment longer.

CHAPTER FOURTEEN

Amy Grimes woke on the morning before her wedding with a raging case of hives.

It had been a long time since she'd had an allergic reaction, though she had learned to control her symptoms by keeping her stress level low and taking time for lots of self care. Amy had definitely *not* been observing either of those necessary lifestyle changes in the past two weeks. She itched and scratched at the angry red welts that were surfacing on her neck as she rummaged through her purse in search of her medicine bag. She fished out her last two non-drowsy allergy chewables and crunched them angrily between her teeth. This was no time to start looking splotchy.

After drinking a big glass of water and brushing her teeth, Amy checked her phone, expecting to see a slew of work emails and messages. She was pleasantly surprised to see that everything was being handled while she was away and there were no fires for her to put out. Even on vacation, Amy always had her phone at the ready in case something went wrong with the software she had built from scratch. ViruSmart was her baby, and like all babies, letting go was hard to do.

Besides the fact that she had a fake marriage to pull off in a little more than twenty-four hours, another source of anxiety had recently manifested for Amy. The overseas tech conglomerate that had been courting her for months had finally sent her an offer she couldn't refuse. Selling her company was something she had never dreamed of when she put her little internet security service together in college. But now, almost a decade later, she had tired of the grind and coming back home had only highlighted her desire to slow down.

With a multi-million dollar offer on the table for her business, the prospect of banking only a half million dollars for basically telling the biggest lie of her entire life seemed even more unreasonable than before. Even though she had yet to look over the offer and knew it would be months before the ink on any kind of contract was dry, the fact was she didn't need this fake wedding for the money anymore. She wanted it.

By the time Amy did her usual morning jog, shower, and breakfast routine, the hives had calmed down and she was starting to look somewhat normal again. She pressed the pale lilac Zac Posen sheath she had purchased for her combination bridal shower/bachelorette party and set her hair in waves for the occasion. Debbie and her mother had planned for a high tea at 4:00 p.m., and then Katie would be taking her out on the town for cocktails afterward. Owen would apparently be lost in the woods with his brother and father and Katie's husband having his own bachelor party.

As Amy put the finishing touches on her look, she realized this was her very last chance to jump. She could give Owen the ring back, apologize to everyone and hop in her car at full speed back to Vero Beach. No harm, no foul. But it wasn't what she really wanted. She wanted to be with Owen. She enjoyed being a part of his family and the way they all so effortlessly embraced her. If she exposed their lie now, would they accept her back in so easily again?

Amy spun the amethyst on her left finger one last time and decided she wasn't ready to give up. Not just yet. She was going to enjoy her tea party and enjoy her last day as Amy Grimes... for a while at least. She was going to allow herself to enjoy the benefits of being Owen Durant's fiancée just one last time.

* * *

After a four-hour long formal high tea and photo session, Katie pulled Amy away from the gathering of women from Debbie's country club and Rhonda's book club, and even a few of Amy's own girlfriends from high school. In short, there were no fewer than fifty women drinking hot tea and munching on cucumber sandwiches, ham salad sandwiches, sausage rolls, petit-fours, and mini pies in the Durant great room that day, and every single one of them were there for her.

"Katie! Why did they invite so many people?" Amy hissed as she was escorted by Owen's sister out the back. "We're only going to have a small ceremony tomorrow!"

"Oh, you know how mother is, she can't resist a good excuse to celebrate," Katie said, the lights of her black BMW SUV blinking as she disarmed it. "You told her you wanted a small wedding and that's what you'll get. You didn't say anything about a small bridal shower."

"I think I have enough negligees and candles to last me a lifetime," Amy laughed as she slid into the passenger seat. "Where are we going?"

"Well, where do you think?" Katie said with a smirk. "The only place in River Ranch worth going to on a Friday night of course."

"*Katie,* not The Watering Trough!" she groaned. "I am *not* dressed for a country-western bar on a Friday night. Look at me! I look like a Stepford Wife."

"You look just fine, I'm all dressed up, too. We'll just get more free drinks is all," she winked.

"Well, I certainly could use a drink," Amy exhaled, staring out the window. "This past two weeks have been such a whirlwind."

"It has," she agreed. "It's been pretty crazy lately with Uncle LeRoy's funeral and everything.

I'm glad that you and Owen are getting married, though. I always wanted to have you as my big sister growing up. Now you will be."

A hot golf ball-sized lump of guilt and regret rose in Amy's throat and tears pricked the corner of her eyes. She pursed her lips together in the dark and tried to swallow it down. Within a few minutes, the bright red and yellow lasso and boots marquee of the bar came into view. Amy sucked in deeply through her nose and prayed that her hives wouldn't return.

Amy shivered and cursed herself once again for forgetting her coat as she stepped out of Katie's warm SUV and into the frosty February night. She rubbed her arms and huddled next to Owen's sister, bracing against the wind as they ran toward the warm beacon of the glowing bar entrance. Twangy music spilled out the double front doors of the establishment over the roar of a hundred laughing, inebriated patrons. As soon as they crossed the threshold, Amy remembered why she tried to stay away from The Watering Trough on the weekends.

"Oh no," she groaned, giving Katie the side-eye. "Line dancing?"

"Yes!" Katie whooped, pumping a fist in the air. "You just need a few shots of tequila and you'll get into it. Let's go!"

Katie grabbed Amy's hand and pulled her to the bar through a sea of sweaty, line dancing bodies. Katie ordered four shots of Patrón Silver and settled in at the bar, clapping her hands in time to the music. The bartender laid out the flight of tequila in front of them, and before Katie could hand over her debit card for the tab, the bartender held up his hand.

"No charge. The gentleman across the way sends his regards."

Amy and Katie both turned their heads to see the flushed, laughing face of Dominic Durant holding up a shot glass in cheers from across the way.

"Dammit, Dom!" Katie shouted, stomping her foot.

Katie shoved two glasses into Amy's hands and double-fisted her own tequila shots before making a beeline to her still laughing brother.

"What the hell, Dominic!" she said, downing her first shot. "I told y'all I was bringing Amy here."

"Dad turned his ankle and had to go home, so we decided to call it a night and just go drinking instead," Dominic shrugged.

"Oh no!" Katie said. "Is he okay?"

"Yeah, he's fine. Mom's probably puttin' ice on it right now," Dominic said, signaling for another round of shots.

"Where's Owen?" Amy asked, searching through the crowd of faces. A hand appeared out of nowhere and snaked around her waist, followed by a breathy voice heavy with tequila.

"Boo!"

Amy whipped around to see Owen, red-faced and clearly drunk as a skunk. She slapped him on the shoulder so hard her hand stung.

"Ow! Hey! Is that any way to greet your fiancé?"

"You scared the life out of me!" Amy said, re-adjusting her dress.

"Come on out and dance with me," Owen insisted, grabbing her by the hand. "They're playing 'Watermelon Crawl.' I know it's your favorite."

"*Fine*," Amy said, rolling her eyes in mock disinterest. He was right. It was her favorite.

Amy followed Owen to the dance floor and took her place in line with more than two dozen other dancing, half-drunk patrons. She was probably the only one there not wearing boots or jeans, but she still remembered the shuffle steps and timing like it was yesterday. After three minutes of two-steps and kick-ball-changes, Amy's forehead was covered in sweat and a smile was plastered across her face.

"Ugh, I need water," Amy panted, fanning herself as they returned to the bar.

"Two waters?" Owen signaled to the bartender. "Where'd Katie and Dom go?"

"Did Nick come with? Maybe they went to find him," she said looking around the bar.

The bartender brought their waters and they chugged them in silence. Amy fanned herself some more as they watched the line dancers keep in time with Alan Jackson's "Chattahoochee."

"Don't they ever play anything new around

this place?" Amy asked, still searching the crowd for Katie.

"Must be oldies night," Owen winked. "Nope. Some things never change."

Owen's face darkened and Amy followed his line of sight to the front entrance. It didn't take long for her to see why his mood suddenly shifted. Tucker strode in through the front door with a date on his arm.

"Well, that's the problem with small towns, I guess," Owen sighed, finishing his water.

Amy's eyes narrowed at the sight of Tucker. Just looking at him made her blood boil. She still felt a bit of guilt for driving a wedge between Owen and his friend. It was nice for Owen to have her back and take her side on the matter just the same.

"We can get out of here if he's bothering you," Amy said, turning away from the entrance. "I don't want to be too trashed for tomorrow any-way."

"No," Owen said, slamming his cup on the counter. "I'm not leaving just because he's here. Be-sides, you need your bull ride first."

Owen looped arms with her and before she could protest, they were two-stepping their way to the corner of the bar that housed the mechanical bull.

"And you can't get out of it because you're wearing some dress!" Owen shouted over the music.

"You go first!" she shouted back.

Owen made a face at her and tipped his hat forward.

"Not a chance."

Amy watched as a familiar shock of red hair swirled in time with the mechanical bull, a fist raised triumphantly in the air. Her mouth opened in a wide, smiling outburst of laughter as she saw Katie mounted high, riding the mechanical bull in her tea time dress like a true pro.

"See," he shrugged, crossing his arms. "You can do it in a dress."

Katie's ride ended with her flushed and laughing hysterically. Nick appeared out of nowhere to help her dismount the mechanical steed like some kind of cartoon princess. Katie spotted them and waved.

"Hey are you going to go?" she yelled out to Amy.

Amy winced and looked back over at Owen, who was positively beaming. He looked like his old, happy self again.

"I'll give it a try," she shrugged.

Owen handed the mechanical bull operator a five-dollar bill and nudged his sister as their impromptu combination bachelor/bachelorette party looked on. Amy ignored the itchy, hot prickling sensation that was creeping up her neck as she carefully placed a foot in the stirrup and slung her leg over the padded saddle. She said a silent prayer of thanks to her earlier self for choosing flats instead of heels that day. With one sweaty palm wrapped firmly around the reins and the other in the air, the bull rocked forward, slowly at first and then faster.

"Heeya!"

A loud, exuberant cry escaped her lips as she bucked too and fro, the blurred faces of her friends and soon-to-be sort of family watching on. After what felt like an eternity, but was probably only a minute, the bull slowed and Owen was at her side helping her dismount. Amy caught her breath and watched as Owen went next, showing off and waving his hat in the air as he rode the bucking mechanical bull. Once everyone had taken their turn, the party returned to the bar for one last round of shots.

"Good to see you can still hold your own, girl," Dominic chided, playfully jabbing Amy in the ribs. "I was worried you were too citified for us anymore."

"Aw, come on," she said. "I'm not really all that different, am I?"

"No," Owen said, smiling down at her with soft eyes. "No you're not."

"To Owen and Amy!" Katie said, raising her shot glass. "Kiss!"

Amy's eyes grew wide as Dominic, Nick, and Katie all chanted kiss, kiss, kiss as they held their shot glasses high. She looked at Owen who was still smiling down at her.

"Guess we have to," she shrugged, her eyes fluttering back up at him.

"Guess so."

Owen leaned in and planted a soft, sweet kiss on her lips as if no one else was there. Amy closed her eyes, determined to remember every moment this time. It seemed like the entire bar around them was cheering, though she barely noticed. All she could think about was how good it felt to be in his arms. How familiar and new he felt all at once, and how she didn't want it to stop. Whether it was the tequila, the dancing, the mechanical bull ride, or just a really good kiss, Owen pulled away and the room spun.

"Wooo!" Dominic called out, patting his brother on the back.

Amy opened her eyes to a dazed looking Owen.

"Shoot, you two," Dominic laughed. "That was some kiss!"

CHAPTER FIFTEEN

Owen didn't sleep a wink the night before the wedding.

He didn't know why he thought this whole scheme would work in the first place. He should have known how his family would react. He should have known how *he* would react. He just didn't count on Amy.

Nursing his third straight hangover in a row, Owen rose on the morning of Valentine's Day with two options: hop on his ATV and disappear into the wilderness forever or marry Amy Grimes. At a quarter past seven, his mother entered his room, opened the blinds, and put a pin in any plans he might have had to escape.

"It's the big day," she said in her no-nonsense voice. "The officiant is going to be here at a quarter to ten. The caterers already dropped off the luncheon and your cake. Did you get your boutonniere from Amy yet?"

Debbie Durant leaned down and planted a kiss on Owen's forehead.

"Woof, you need a shower. Hurry up," she said, patting his knee. "I hung your suit in the closet."

Owen pulled the covers back over his head and groaned. As he laid in bed watching sun stream in through his window, Owen could only think about how soon, he would be kissing Amy again, but this time, as her lawfully wedded husband. And then what? Then he would have to endure a three-day honeymoon in New Orleans trying to pretend the whole time that he didn't want to be with her? Owen didn't even want to think about what would happen after.

It wasn't supposed to go this way, he thought to himself, finally getting out of bed. *I wasn't supposed to feel like this.*

Still, with the prospect of his future plans for Camp Durant on the line, Owen resigned himself to the mess he had made. He knew there was nothing he could do now but shower, shave, get dressed, and hope he wasn't about to make the biggest mistake of his entire life.

❊ ❊ ❊

Amy didn't sleep a wink the night before the wedding.

Her hives returned full-force after her Watering Trough kiss with Owen and she was all out of antihistamines. As the sun finally rose, Amy escaped her parents' house to the only twenty-four hour pharmacy in River Ranch and procured a new supply of allergy medicine. As she stared out into the still, chilly Valentine's Day morning, Amy realized that all she had to do was get in her car and drive back to Vero Beach. Sure, she would be a runaway bride, but she would also be free of the neverending lies and guilt. She would be free from the way she felt about Owen. The way she *really* felt.

Still, as her allergy meds kicked in, Amy began to relax and was able to think straight again. This was the end. After today, she and Owen would celebrate at Mardi Gras and forget the whole thing. He would have the access to the funds he needed to start his non-profit, and she would... well, what *would* she do?

Owen had been right about one thing; she *did* want to travel more. Selling ViruSmart and retiring early would make her adventures even more enjoyable. She was getting sick of being tied to her work email all the time. But even for someone as independent as Amy had been for so long, traveling alone can get boring and lonely after a while. She had long thought it would be nice to have someone to travel with and a place to set down roots. She had been convinced for so long that being in a long-term, committed relationship could never make her happy. Somehow, Owen Durant had rattled her brain and dredged enough feelings to the surface to make her reconsider everything she used to think about relationships and herself.

Amy pushed aside her wedding day jitters and decided not to run away after all. She had a hair and makeup appointment in just a few hours and still needed to pick up her flowers and get dressed. Her father would be wearing a suit and tie for the first time since she could remember, and she couldn't even begin to imagine how much money the Durant family had spent for their small affair. Running away would disappoint far too many people now, not least of all, Owen. If she really did love him — and after their kiss the night before she was pretty positive that she did — leaving him at the altar, fake wedding or not, would be a horrible thing to do.

As Amy headed back toward home, she reminisced about the last couple of weeks she had spent with Owen. Despite all the time that had passed and their opposing lifestyles, deep down, their bond was still intact. There was something between them that she had never experienced with anyone else; something intangible and unnamed. That special something was never more obvious than when they were together, and for the past two weeks, it almost felt like those summers long ago. Owen made her feel happy and free. He made her feel like a kid again. And that was a feeling Amy wasn't ready to let go of just yet.

❋ ❋ ❋

"Well, don't you look sharp as a tack?"

Dominic slapped Owen on the back as he stood under the giant oak in the backyard of his family estate just on the outskirts of their hundreds of acres of property. Two dozen white folding chairs encircled the spot; seats that would soon be filled with smiling, familiar faces looking up at him expectantly. It was five minutes past eleven and the Justice of the Peace he had hired only the week before stared at her watch with a twinge of worry. Owen hadn't heard from Amy since 8:00 a.m. when she said she was going to get her hair done and he was starting to worry himself.

"I just saw Amy and her mother in the kitchen," Dom said, readjusting his belt buckle. "Apparently there was some kinda issue with the flowers. Katie had to run and pick a bouquet of flowers from the garden right quick."

"Oh," Owen said, exhaling deeply. He hadn't realized he was holding his breath. "Okay."

Just then, Amy's father emerged from the back door of the house in step with his own father. The two men smiled at each other and shook hands as they took their seats under the shade of the oak tree and Owen felt his heart sink once again. In just a few minutes he was going to lie in front of both of them. It was a lie he was going to have to live with for the rest of his life.

Katie hurried out the back door of the estate, followed by Rhonda and Martin. The poolhouse surround sound system kicked in and the first chords of the traditional bridal march echoed throughout the Durant family property, signaling that the wedding was about to begin.

And that's when he saw her.

Amy Grimes, the girl he used to scamper through the woods behind his house with. The girl who fell out of the very tree he was standing under. The girl who had grown to be the smartest, most independent, most beautiful woman he had ever met, was walking his way. She was an angel in cream-colored lace, clutching a haphazard bouquet of his mother's pink tea roses. It was an image he would remember forever. An image that stabbed him deep in the heart; a pain that hurt and felt so good all at once.

As she neared the seated guests, Amy's father rose to greet her and took her by the arm. They made the last leg of the journey to the end of the aisle together as father and daughter, Owen grinning and holding back the urge to cry all the way. But before Owen could gather his thoughts, Amy was at his side, her hands were in his, warm and solid and real. He could feel the cold, hard weight of his grandmother's engagement band beneath his fingers as he looked into Amy's eyes.

She had that look again. It was a look he didn't see often in her eyes, but he had seen it before, in that very same spot in fact, some twenty years ago. It was the same look that was in her eyes when she fell out of the tree and couldn't breathe for what felt like an eternity. It was the look of fear.

"Amy," he said, squeezing her hand.

But before Owen could say another word, the officiant began and their wedding ceremony was officially underway.

❋ ❋ ❋

"Is my hair too high?"

Amy regarded herself in the hall mirror adjacent to the great room at the Durant estate, not one bit happy with the person looking back. It was the morning of her wedding and anything that could go wrong, had. She should have taken it as a sign; that getting married the day after Friday the Thirteenth, on Valentine's Day, without her best friend and under false pretenses was just a no good, very bad idea. But Amy continued to not listen to her instincts like she usually did. She was going against every grain of good sense in her body and she was doing it for Owen. And now, she was going to be late for her own fake wedding.

"There's no such thing as hair that's too high," her mother said, kissing her on the cheek. "You look beautiful."

Amy's shoulders fell. She fussed with her veil again.

"Got 'em!"

Katie burst through the back door, breathless with a bouquet of pink tea roses in her hand. She let out a big "phew!" and handed the flowers to Amy.

"I am so sorry that Cookie ate your calla lilies," Amy's mother cringed.

"Oh, it's alright," Amy said, admiring the quickie bouquet. "I almost like these better."

"We are running late. Do you have everything you need?" Katie asked, checking the time on her phone.

"Yes, I think I'm ready," Amy said, poking at the bobby pins that attached the veil to her head.

"You stand at the back door and wait," Owen's mother instructed. "I'll start the music and you just walk down toward the old oak. That's where we've got everything set up."

"The old oak!"

Amy gathered her lace mermaid skirt and walked over to the back window overlooking the wide expanse of Durant property. Sure enough, there was Owen, dressed in a smart black tux with no hat in sight standing under the tree. *Their* tree. Her lower lip jutted out as she pursed her lips together. Hot, salty tears began to well up around her perfectly applied mascara despite her efforts to hold them back.

"Oh, don't you start blubberin' now," her mother said, coming to her aid with a Kleenex. "We didn't pay Bobbie Sue seventy-five dollars to fix your makeup so you can cry it all off."

Rhonda Grimes dabbed her own eyes and gave her daughter a hug.

"Are you going to be okay?"

Amy sniffed and nodded.

"Your dad will be waiting for you at the end of the aisle. Good luck, Sweetie."

With that, her mother slipped out the back door, still sniffling, leaving Amy alone for her last moment as an unmarried woman in the quiet, empty estate. Amy looked down at the ring on her finger and wondered what Owen's grandmother would have thought of all this. She laughed through her nose, wondering what *Uncle LeRoy* would have thought. She stared out the window again, past her waiting groom, past the oak tree, past the treeline to the rooftop of her grandparents' house. She wondered what *they* would have thought of this whole thing.

A blast of organ music from the outdoor stereo system jarred her from her thoughts. There was no more time to consider the what-ifs. No more time to worry. It was time for her to do the thing she promised she would do all along. It was time for her to marry Owen Durant.

The bridal march blasted in her ears as she clutched her quickie bouquet. Two dozen pairs of eyes stared up at her expectantly as she tried to smile and not trip over her long, lacy train. It was a beautiful, crisp February morning; the prettiest Valentine's Day she could remember in a long time. It would have been a perfect day to get married if the nuptials were real.

Amy trained her eyes on Owen as she made her way down the aisle. His chosen wedding attire was much different than she had imagined; no hat, no jeans. No boots even. In his slick rented tux and shiny black shoes, Owen Durant looked more like a double agent than a cowhand-turned-IT-professional. Seeing him so dressed up — so grown-up looking — made her smile. He had come a long way from the skinny kid she used to know, and the cocky teen that once turned her away. But underneath the expensive rented tux, everything that made him Owen still shined through like a beacon, pointed straight at her. In that moment, Amy knew that no matter what happened after that day, he would always and forever be in her life. How could he not be?

Jeff Grimes hoisted himself from the foldout chair at the back of the aisle as she approached, looking sharper than he had in years. Her father had even shaved for the occasion, and Amy smiled as she took his arm. This moment was one of the reasons she had refused to allow herself to run that morning. Even if the moment wasn't going to last, even if the wedding wasn't real, Amy was able to share this one special memory with her father. Nothing could take that away. Even a little white lie.

Amy's cheeks began to sting with permagrin as her father delivered her in front of the officiant and a now visibly worried Owen. In the time it had taken her to take her father's arm and walk the two dozen or so steps to the altar, Owen's demeanor had changed from exuberant to downright anxious. Amy could tell something was wrong, but

Owen took her hand and the officiant began the ceremony just the same.

Are you okay? she mouthed to him, but he wasn't looking at her. His eyes were open wide, darting wildly to the wedding guests and the officiant and then back at Amy again. A thin sheen of sweat started to form on his forehead. He looked how she felt inside.

"Amy," he said, clearing his throat. He squeezed her hands harder. Amy's stomach did a somersault as the officiant droned on.

"Amy, I don't want to marry you."

CHAPTER SIXTEEN

Amy's legs went numb and a shot of adrenaline raced up her spine as the words "I don't want to marry you" fell from her faux financé's lips. She and Owen hadn't exactly planned what they were going to say at the altar; the Justice of the Peace brought a generic set of vows for them to read, so she hadn't bothered practicing anything. But there was one thing that was for sure; what Owen just said out loud in front of everyone was *not* on the script.

"What?" she whispered.

"I don't want to marry you," he said, still holding her hands. "I can't."

"Owen, don't do this," she said, her gaze drawn to the dozen pairs of eyes staring back at them. Amy looked to the officiant for help but she was just as bewildered as the bride.

"Amy, I don't want to marry you because I love you."

Amy blinked and any sensation that may have been lingering in her limbs disappeared.

"I've always loved you," he continued.

"Wait," she shook her head, sucking in a deep breath. "I don't understand."

"I'm trying to say that I love you but I don't want us to live a lie. We don't need to do this."

A rush of warmth flooded from her chest down to her toes, reviving her dead limbs. Her pulse beat faster at that moment then on her morning jogs. Her heart felt fuller in that moment then when she was securing a business deal or landing in a strange new place. Her whole being glowed, all because of three little words.

"Owen," she smiled. "I love you, too."

He let out a loud sigh of relief and half-smiled as he put a hand to his head.

"But what about the deal," she whispered, her eyes darting back to their wedding guests and the officiant again.

"Fuck the deal," he grinned.

"Are you sure about this?"

"Positive."

"Well then, so am I."

Owen wrapped an arm around her waist and pulled her in, kissing her harder and truer than anyone had ever kissed her in her entire life. Relief washed over her whole being as she lost herself in that kiss, to the sound of gasps from the wedding party and the officiant clearing her throat.

"Excuse me," the Justice of the Peace cut in. "We generally reserve the kiss for *after* the bride and groom say 'I do'?"

"I'm sorry, folks," Owen said, his arms still wrapped tight around her waist. "Amy and I have something to announce. We never really wanted to get married."

Another round of gasps and questioning murmurs sounded from the row of foldout chairs. The Justice of the Peace threw up her hands.

"What Owen is trying to say is," Amy cut in. "We just aren't ready to get married yet."

Amy's eyes darted to her parents. She was worried she would disappoint them the most of all. To her surprise, Rhonda and Jeff Grimes were both looking at each other and smiling.

"I just don't understand," Owen's mother said from the front row. "You love each other... but you don't want to get married?"

"I'm sorry, Mom," Owen said, breaking away from his now ex-fiancée. He wrapped his mother in a hug as she looked on quizzically. Owen shook his father's hand.

"We'll explain everything when we get back."

Owen returned to the altar and looked up into the boughs of the great shady oak overhead. He extended his hand to Amy, looking impossibly more handsome and happy than ever.

"Shall we, Miss Grimes?"

Amy smiled and looked down at her best friend. At the love of her life.

"Let's get the hell out of here."

Amy slipped her hand in his, gathered her

lace skirt, and took off toward Owen's black truck parked just in the distance.

"I'm sorry, Mr. and Mrs. Durant!" she called over her shoulder. "Thank you so much for everything!"

Amy kissed her mother and father on the cheek on the way out, promising to call them. She took one last whiff of Debbie Durant's tea rose bouquet and tossed it to Katie, who was shaking her head as a smirk playing out on her lips.

"Goodbye everyone, we love you!" Amy called back, making a beeline for the truck.

Owen tore off his bow-tie and suit jacket as they closed in on the truck, only stopping to open the door for Amy. He kissed her one last time, briefly, but full of more pure, unadulterated joy than ever before.

"Where to?" he asked, helping her up into the truck. She tore off her organza and tulle veil and tossed it on the ground. Owen slid into the driver's side of the truck and looked at her, panting and covered in a layer of perspiration.

"It's about a fourteen-hour drive to New Orleans," she said, her forehead lined with hesitation. "Do you think you can make it?"

Owen revved his engine and squeezed her hand. He nodded and threw his F-150 into reverse.

"Hell yes, I can."

CHAPTER SEVENTEEN

"Woooo!"

Amy Grimes leaned over the balcony of their hotel room, a foot-long glass of fruity, alcohol-laden Hurricane in one hand and a collection of beads clutched in the other. A familiar arm snaked its way around her waist, pulling her away from the wrought-iron railing as a green and gold float ambled down Bourbon Street below. Cheers from drunken tourists and jazz music floated up from the street below as he spun her around and planted the hundredth kiss on her lips that day.

"You were 'bout to fall over, girl."

"Was not," she said, playfully slapping him on the arm. "This isn't my first rodeo, you know. I do Mardi Gras every year."

"Well, I can certainly see the appeal," he said, hugging her from behind as they enjoyed the scenery below.

"Is your mom still mad?" Amy cringed, looking up at him over her shoulder. He kissed her forehead tenderly in reply.

"She'll get over it. She's more upset that she was left with ten pounds of shrimp salad and a $400 wedding cake, but that's her fault. We tried to tell them we didn't want to make the ceremony a big deal."

"I just don't want your family to be angry with me," she said. "I know we did the right thing but I still feel a little guilty."

"Dominic told me he knew all along," Owen said, stealing a sip of her drink. "Called me a dumb-ass and said he and Katie would have helped me with the foundation, Uncle LeRoy be damned."

"Shhh!" Amy said, slapping him on the arm again. "Don't speak ill of the dead like that! Plus, I actually have to thank your Uncle LeRoy. If he didn't put that silly clause in his will, we wouldn't be standing here right now."

"Hmm," Owen laughed through his nose. "Almost seemed by design didn't it? Like this was all meant to be. "

"Maybe it was," she said, staring dreamily into the crowd. "I'm glad we didn't get married. It's much better this way."

Owen nodded.

"You're right. Plus, we still got to have our honeymoon," he said, gently pinching her waist. "I don't know why I was so afraid to leave home before. This is really nice."

"Well, I'm glad you gave it a chance," Amy said, waving down to the crowd.

"I'm sorry I won't have that half a million for

you for a while," Owen sighed. "I'll get it to you, though. A promise is a promise."

"I don't need it anymore," Amy shrugged. "I'm selling ViruSmart. I got an offer from an overseas buyer this morning. All I have to do is sign."

"What!" Owen said, holding up his palm for a high-five. She slapped it back, giving him a smirk. Even though they were lovers now, they were always going to be friends first. "Hot damn, you're going to be richer than me now!" he laughed.

"Maybe," Amy shrugged.

"Maybe I should have married you after all," he said, hugging her from behind again. "I could enjoy being a rich, stay-at-home husband."

"Not likely. You would get bored in a second and you know it."

Amy and Owen held each other and stared down at the stream of revealing parade participants and enjoyed a quiet moment of silence. Amy spun the amethyst ring around her finger; she had gotten so used to wearing it, she forgot to take it off.

"I guess I should give this back to you," she shrugged, tugging the purple stone from her finger. "We don't have to pretend to be engaged anymore."

"Keep it," he said, placing it back on her finger. "It suits you."

Amy smirked at him and turned the ring around on her finger again. He was right. It did suit her.

"So what next, Mr. Durant? Go home and face the music?" Amy said, inhaling a deep breath of New Orleans air.

"We could just keep on runnin'," he said, placing a protective arm around her shoulder. "We could forget everything and you could show me the world."

"That's a really nice dream," she replied, closing her eyes.

"*You* were my dream," he said, this time without a hint of sarcasm.

"I love you, Owen. I really do."

"Not as much as I love you, Amy Grimes."

"Always?"

"Always," he replied, kissing the top of her head. "You're the one thing I'm in no hurry to get over."

ABOUT THE AUTHOR

Wendy Dalrymple is a professional copywriter living in sunny Tampa Bay, FL. When she's not writing, you can find her camping with her family, painting bad wall art, trying to grow pineapples, learning '90s radio hits to play on her ukulele, or walking her dog. Keep up with Wendy at www.wendydalrymple.com!

BOOKS BY THIS AUTHOR

Miss Claus And The Millionaire

Nicole Myers loves making and selling crafts in her spare time, and her greatest wish is to turn her booming Etsy business into something bigger. Nicole's hand-painted Russian nesting dolls have become a hit at the morning market in downtown St. Petersburg, FL, and to her surprise, her work even lands her in the local newspaper. Nicole wants nothing more than to use her platform as an artist to help raise awareness for kids in need during the holidays and all year long, but, as with all good causes, what she really needs is money.

Roman Regan is rich and good-looking, but despite his chiseled features and big bank account, he's also very lonely. Christmas was never really fun for Roman growing up; for an only child who always got everything he ever wanted, the holidays didn't hold any special meaning. When Nicole and her nesting dolls catch his eye, he is reminded of something he loved and lost long ago. Roman becomes determined to get his hands on one of Nicole's hand-made toys... and maybe get his hands on her in the process.

Kissing Christmas Goodbye

Full of Christmas wonder, eggnog, and endearing characters, Wendy Darlymple's Kissing Christmas Goodbye is a charming tale of getting a second chance at love. Christmas is Lizzy's favorite time of year; even when divorcing her husband forced her and her daughter to move back in with Lizzy's parents. Max hates Christmas and all the pomp and candy canes that goes with it. What's worse is the house he's renovating is smack dab in the middle of the uber festive Candy Cane Lane. Just when Lizzy thinks she can convince her grinchy neighbor Max to participate in the neighborhood-wide decorating, her world is threatened when Lizzy's ex demands their daughter spend Christmas with him and the other woman.

Chasin' Jason

Jason Valentine is all that Luna Lloyd can think about. Once a week, the enchanting entrepreneur stops into Luna's printing shop, Copy Cats, to make copies, mail promotional materials and check his reflection in the mirror. Against her better judgement, Luna does a deep dive into Jason's online presence, only to find herself becoming more infatuated with her enchanting out-of-reach customer every day.

Armin is Luna's best friend and the owner of Barks Books, the used book shop and café next door. He harbors a secret crush on his friend and business neighbor, but hides his feelings behind a cup of coffee and a stack of books. Armin knows that Jason is all wrong for Luna, but he tries to be a good friend and keep his opinions to himself just the same.

When Luna finally works up the nerves to talk to the mysterious, hunky Jason, she gets more than she bargains for, and finds herself invited to one of his events. Of course, she asks Armin to come along as her wingman, which only makes him loathe his romantic rival even more. Comedy ensues as Luna chases after the man of her dreams with Armin right at her heels, only to find that the true love of her life might have been right in front of her face all along.

Tamsen's Hollow

Tamsen Hayes vowed never to return to her hometown of Franklin, North Carolina. But then again, she never thought she would lose her job and end her relationship on the same day, either. Weary of the hustle and bustle of corporate work and city life and in need of a new place to live, Tamsen impulsively purchases a fixer-upper farm that she had always admired as a child. With a few coats of colorful paint, and the addition of a few adorable goats, her little farm in the holler starts to feel like home.What she didn't bet on was that a handsome neighbor with a mysterious past would come with the territory. Despite their friendship and mutual attraction, Tamsen just can't seem to shake the memories of her ex, and finds herself building a wall and running away before she gets hurt by anyone... especially the enigmatic Jake Turner. Tamsen soon learns that if she can't move on, she might end up closing the door on something good and missing out on an unexpected love that, just maybe, was always meant to be.

Revolve: A Bewitching Romance

Jessica Marx is a full-time shop girl and a part-time witch living among the mortals in Ybor City, Florida. She uses her powers of divination and enchantment to help deserving customers at her boutique find love, turning special articles of vintage clothing into time machines, portals to other dimensions, and wearable glamour spells. Even though she's still a new witch, her love spells seem to work (sort of) and Jessica gets a boost of good vibes every time she helps make a love connection. Too bad Jessica can't conjure a love spell for herself...

Made in the USA
Monee, IL
15 January 2022

88969932R00100